ALL IN

D.C. Knights Book 3

JUNO CHASE

Copyright © 2017 by Juno Chase

All rights reserved.

No part of this book may be reproduced in any form or by any electronic or mechanical means, including information storage and retrieval systems, without written permission from the author, except for the use of brief quotations in a book review.

This is a work of fiction. Any similarities to real people is made up. Some of the places are real, but the events taking places at them are fiction.

ISBN: 978-1-947234-04-8

Print ISBN: 978-1-947234-21-5

You believe this is a game,
And you may be right.
But, if you think you can
play it better than me, think
again.

—Anon

Chapter 1

$\mathcal{M}$adeline placed the government issued laptop into her vintage leather bag. She traced a finger along the letters of her surname on the brass tag-ASHER. Her grandfather had owned this years ago, probably never imagining it might carry a computer. It had come to her with a worn dignity and suppleness to the leather that she found comforting.

She made sure that Congressman Pierce's office was empty. She liked to be the last to leave. As his communications director, she had invitations to four different events that evening. None of them were required, and she was blowing them off in order to go home and relax.

The Metro ride from Capitol Hill to DuPont circle was packed, but a cute guy in a kilt gave up his seat for her. Madeline swung by the Chinese takeout shop on the corner of her block to grab dinner. Finally home, she took off her high heels, opened a fresh bottle of Perrier, and dug her chopsticks into her General Tso's chicken.

A printed BINGO card lay on her cement kitchen countertop. The women in her office had actually agreed to her little BINGO scheme. She'd tossed it out there in the spur of the moment, to liven things up. The idea was pretty simple—be the first to kiss five different men at five different monuments around DC to fill out a line on the card. And, they had agreed to play along.

The winner of their little game would accompany Congressman Pierce to Las Vegas to a charity fundraiser. Yawn. But, the real prize would be partaking in a secret meeting, code named SUNFLOWER, with media-prime entrepreneurs. Her career trajectory would point sky-high—without her parents' influence. That was the kind of challenge Madeline wanted.

She planned to win and already had two BINGO kisses. Monday night she had met an AP photographer at a bar within an hour of starting the game. First kiss. Today was a fortuitous lunch with a lobbyist she'd set up weeks ago. Second kiss. Tomorrow morning, she had a coffee-date with an analyst from the CIA. Third kiss. Three kisses in as many days? A win was practically guaranteed if she kept up this pace.

Her phone flashed with a new call, her sister. Madeline preferred to video chat, but Aundrea refused. She had a six-month-old daughter, Ava---her sweet little niece---who grabbed the phone, resulting in zero conversation. She slid the answer button.

"Darling, you must come up this weekend."

The Bluetooth connection wasn't great, and she rolled her eyes. Aundrea had two nannies, a full-time housekeeper, a toddler sleep consultant, and a 'toddler concierge' who designed their ergonomic nursery and selected appropriate toys for brain development. Couldn't the nanny watch Ava so they could video conference?

"Bunny and Skip are throwing a fundraiser party. They just bought a new place in East Hampton, did you know? It's off the water, of course. While it certainly isn't the party of the year, it will be amazing."

"Let me check my schedule, hold on." A large goal was posted above her day planner: WIN BINGO. "Sorry. I can't. I need to take care of something this weekend."

"What do you have more important than your sister? Now, be a good girl and come visit? Ava misses her favorite aunt."

"Aw, Ava. I do miss my little niece. Let me see if I

can set something up." Madeline clicked on the Match icon. She quickly scrolled down a list of men.

"Do you want me to call you back?"

"No," Madeline said. Her sister had a sixth sense about being ignored. "Just a minute." If she could set up a fourth date before the weekend, then she'd go. That way her fourth BINGO kiss would be set up and she could relax in New York City.

"Madeline. Come on. What are you doing?"

"I'm arranging plans so that I can come see you." She stopped scrolling when she saw a picture of a good-looking man with dark hair and a strong jawline. She clicked on his profile. Jack was perfect. He was a corporate litigation lawyer. Based on his profile, he looked easy to kiss and release.

She sent him a private message. Most men didn't take very long to respond to her. She had thick brown hair down to the middle of her back, her body was naturally thin, thanks to her mother's genetics and her years of fencing. Her balletic lunge and recover skills and her lofty grades had earned her a full-ride scholarship at Berkeley. Four years later, she graduated magna cum laude. With a resume like hers, not many men said *no. Prime Grade Arm Candy.*

"Check. Now to the important question dear sister, how am I going to get to New York? I'd rather not take the train."

"Don't worry. I'll check with Dave and we'll get you on a jet, maybe Bunny and Skip's. I'll have my driver pick you up at La Guardia."

"Will I get to spend time with Ava? Or is it all about the party?"

"I promise you will get to spend time with Ava. Come up Thursday night. We'll have a nice dinner. On Friday, we'll head up to the Hamptons. I've rented a house for the evening since Ava and Emily, the nanny, are coming with us. You'll be back by Sunday afternoon in DC."

"Hold on. Let me check." Madeline looked at the phone to check her calendar and emails. Nothing from Jack yet, but, to be fair, it had only been two minutes.

Madeline smiled as she sipped her water. The game was a testament to how resourceful and organized she was. Her mother would be proud. She glanced at her work emails. Her Pavlovian response was to open the email without regard to Aundrea still on the phone. *I'll be fast.* She clicked the reply button to an email and started typing.

"Oh, my God! You are just like Mom. I can hear you typing. Stop working and talk to me."

It wasn't the first time Aundrea had said something like that. "I'm just like Mom? Oh, and you and your fifty nannies is not like Mom at all. Nope."

"Oh stop it. You have no idea how hard it is to be a

mom. I didn't sleep for six weeks. And I'm doing a Mommy and Me class with Ava, a drum class that is helping me and Ava connect on a primal, musical level. Being a mom is hard work. Not that you would know."

"Especially when someone else does it for you."

"Come on Madeline. I don't want to argue tonight. I am doing my best. I'm more involved than mom ever was. I'm staying home with Ava. She knows me."

"You're right. I'm sorry. You're right. Mom worked insane hours, she still does. I think she made it to one of my tournaments. Maybe two."

"I know, right? Never saw her at a soccer game without a Blackberry in her face. I'm not sure she ever saw me make a goal. Sometimes I wanted to smash that stupid phone of hers."

"The double-edged sword of technology. Oh, I forgot to tell you. Dad is here in DC for six weeks. Mom says she didn't realize his midlife crisis would take ten years when he bought the winery. I guess he hired a new master winemaker from MIT to come in. Some bohemian chemist who grew up in France."

"Yeah, I heard at Thanksgiving. I served his chardonnay for a dinner party, and Bunny loved it. She's having it brought in special for the Hampton's party. Another reason you have to come. Dad's wine will be there. We have to support him."

"You never give up, do you? I'm glad he bought the winery. You know, he started coming to my matches after that."

"Me too. I just, I don't know. It's Dad, you know," Aundrea said.

Madeline could almost hear her sister's eyes rolling.

"What is he doing in DC, anyway?" Aundrea asked.

"He's here for a charity project, to help build a new app for food banks. Mom said he's taking a cooking class too."

"Charity's good. Cooking is weird. Do you think he'll ever go back to San Francisco?" She didn't wait for an answer but plowed on. "Maybe they should get divorced. I don't know... let's talk about that when you get here."

Whether or not their parents might get a divorce had been an increasingly frequent topic of conversation with her sister. Madeline knew the situation between her parents was not normal. Her dad had moved to Napa when she was a junior in high school, and her mom stayed in the City and continued her job as CMO for Global Tech.

They spent summers at the winery and the school year in San Francisco with Mom. Madeline had always expected her dad to move back, or that her mom would move down to join him at the winery. Ten years later, they were still flying back and forth. "Who knows when Mom and Dad are going to do anything. They are so stubborn. It didn't help that you changed your name either. Was it all to frustrate Mama bear? Get back at Dad?"

"Knock it off. There was no subterfuge involved, really Madeline. I simply liked it better. Sounded European. I thought it was cool. I still do."

"I thought Mom was going to lose it. Anyway, you'll always be Andrea to me."

"You only call me that when you want to make fun of me. I have no reason to go back to plain ol' Andrea."

"Okay, okay Aundrea. New topic. Maybe you're right. Maybe I should come up and see the sweetest niece ever. I miss her."

"Is that a yes? The sleep consultant is coming over tonight. But I wanted to call Rosa first and see how she got us hooligans to sleep at night."

"My appearance is a solid maybe. I miss Rosa. Give her my love." Madeline twirled her hair. How hard could the parenting thing really be? Was a sleep consultant and two nannies really necessary for one six-month-old? She didn't want to have someone else raise her kids.

Even though she'd started out as another nanny, Rosa had stayed around undaunted by Madeline's and

Aundrea's shenanigans. She had become so much more to both of them. Did her mother have a clue what place Rosa had in both their hearts? Was she ever jealous?

Madeline wasn't sure she could be a mom, either. It didn't look easy. Who knows? And when she considered the realities of her life---no boyfriend and an exciting work life---did the specifics of how she wanted to raise her hypothetical kids matter? Aundrea was a good mom and having help let her be a better mom. And yes, Aundrea was there for her daughter. Her intentions were honorable.

"Thank God for that woman. I wish she would move to New York and help me with Ava."

"Why won't she?"

"Her grandkids keep her close. Plus, she's helping Dad out at the winery managing the housekeepers and grounds. She keeps everyone in line, just like she used to us."

"She's perfect for that job. If it weren't for her, neither of us would know Spanish. I feel bad I haven't spoken in a while."

"Even in DC? I would've thought you'd have plenty of opportunity."

"I did, when you were working as a translator for the UN and came down to visit. Since you don't visit as much as you used to, it's mostly chance that I run into the Latino crowd."

"I do miss working." Ava started to cry in the background, a loud, lusty cry with a piercing need. "Ava, hold on. I'll be there in a second. EMILY! Grab Ava for me! Oh Madeline. Some days, I desperately want to go back to work."

"It doesn't have to be like our parents. You could find something."

"I know, but I don't want it to be like that. They were always at work. And with babies---there is no balance. They need you all the time. That's what makes the decision to go back to work so hard." Soft fabric rustled and Ava stopped crying, ratcheting down to a whimper. "Now, before I go, Dave told me there will be some hot single guys there. It won't be one of those boring married people parties. I promise."

Madeline checked the status on her private message to Jack on Match. He still hadn't responded. "Tell me why Bunny is throwing the party again."

"You know Dave volunteers in Central America every year for a couple weeks as part of the Orthopedics Every Family Foundation. Anyway, Bunny and Skip run the foundation. The young men are mostly doctors who volunteer with their time, but they also need to raise money for travel and hotels."

Madeline twirled a pen in her hand. *A boring long-*

winded fundraiser. "I wish I could, but there's another party I'm supposed to go to this weekend."

"There are a million parties in DC. There is only one party with your sister. It takes place in New York."

"There's a different reason I need to stay in DC."

"What could be more important than your sister and Ava?"

Madeline opened her mouth, about to explain the BINGO game, but then shut it. She didn't want to say anything. It was one thing to play the BINGO game when it sounded fun and flirty, but it was entirely different to explain the game to her sister without sounding slutty. She rationalized the game, it wasn't slutty, it was just a couple of kisses, but still, she couldn't keep a secret from her sister. "If I tell you, you have to promise you won't tell anyone. Not even Dave."

"Are you kidding me? What? C'mon just tell me. ... Okay, I promise."

"Pinky promise?"

"I pinky promise."

"There's this important meeting coming up in Vegas, and only one of us can go. All of us are qualified to go, so instead of just picking one person arbitrarily, we are playing a game of kiss and tell. We're calling it Monument BINGO."

"What does that even mean?"

"Well, you find a guy with a certain job and you have to kiss him in a predetermined place, like the Washington Monument. Every girl has a BINGO card. The first person to get BINGO wins and gets to go to Vegas."

"Are you kidding me? That's the stupidest thing I ever heard. You have to kiss five guys? In how long?"

"Two weeks."

"Did you think up this game?"

Madeline nearly dropped her phone. "How did you know?"

"You did this in college. How many guys will buy me a drink? How many guys will take me on a date? Mom really fucked up the way we think about relationships. You make the game sound so business-like, you know a means to an end. Knowing you, there's probably a spreadsheet involved."

"There is no a spreadsheet. It's not that complicated. Frankly, I was surprised when the other girls went for it. I didn't think they would. When Liz agreed to play, I was shocked."

"I remember Liz. If I know her, I am positive she didn't agree to play any game. She probably went along with the game to shut you up, you know, to placate you and your stubborn drive. I'm sure you showed up with BINGO card samples, the rules, and exactly how to win the prize. I'd bet Daddy's winery that you made damn sure there was no chance to say no."

"Who me? Besides, I'm going to get my fourth kiss this week. By Friday night, I promise you, I will win."

"There is more to life than playing ridiculous dating games. Like love."

"Love is nothing but a series of chemicals released into brain matter. A synapse has fired and dopamine is dumped. Yay love."

"Don't you think you'll fall in love someday?"

"Me? Nah. You got lucky. Dave is awesome." Madeline didn't believe love was her destiny; she had too many asshole ex's. Love wanted nothing to do with her. Love was not in the stars for her.

"Someday, you just wait. Someday it'll hit you right between the eyes. You've got to let the past go hon."

Madeline didn't respond. Past relationships had left an uncomfortable ache inside her. Two years with Aaron in high school, and he dumped her right after the homecoming game, calling her a bitch in front of everyone. Damon in college; he cheated on her. Then a string of physically satisfying, but emotionally draining lovers in DC followed. She had so much hope for each man that the casual relationship would bloom into something more. But it never worked out.

Love ain't happening here. Her phone vibrated

with a new message. She checked the email header, and it was from Jack, the guy from Match. She had scored a date.

"I've got a date. A BINGO kiss."

"Set it up for Wednesday, or even tonight. Then you'll have how many Bingos?"

"I have a coffee date tomorrow morning. A date with Jack in the evening. Now, if I can set up one more date for Thursday or Friday, I'll win."

"And the deadline is when?"

Madeline glanced at the calendar. "Thirteen days."

"Skip Thursday. You're way ahead in the game then. Come to New York Thursday night. When you're here, you can set up a date in DC on Tinder or whatever it is you kids are using these days, and you'll win BINGO by Monday morning. Besides, you'll ruin the fun for the other girls if you win on Friday."

"You sound like Mom."

"I know. But it works with you."

"It's just a kiss Aundrea."

"Someday you'll find a guy and want to have his babies. But if not, you know, just keep playing your games."

"Going deep Aundrea," Madeline said, warning her.

"Dave just texted me. Bunny is in DC and chartering a plane. I'll get you a ride. You're coming to New York."

"Alright. I'll come. Will you make me your home-made macaroni?"

"You know I will. Gruyere, Cheddar, and Provolone. Thursday night darling."

Chapter 2

The Congressional Coffee Shop was mostly empty this time of morning. Madeline needed some extra caffeine before she met up with Liz. Not that she needed caffeine to be around Liz, but rather she had gotten up early to have a sunrise date with her third kiss, the CIA analyst at the Arlington Memorial. It was a little awkward and not very romantic, but a kiss was a kiss was a kiss. Her fourth BINGO kiss would be with Jack after work. *Was it wrong to have two dates in one day?*

She ordered a skinny-vanilla-spice-dirty-chai-latte. Liz would be there any minute. Due to the mercurial state of political affairs, they would be lucky to get five minutes before a meeting or important call would pop up. That was the price of being a civil servant. Dave, her brother-in-law, had joked that she was like a doctor, but she didn't get to save anyone's life. Madeline saved lives in other ways, and she didn't expect everyone to see that. She was good at her job. But that meant she was always ready to jump in and solve problems, always ready with answers.

Madeline sat down at a small table and kept her ears open to the surrounding conversation, just in case someone dropped a tasty tidbit. *You never know.* She heard nothing but dinner plans and generic statements like 'I'm so busy!' 'No one sleeps on the Hill' or they talked in code with such general references that gleaning true meaning would be difficult if not impossible.

No one ever talked politics at the coffee shop, even the interns knew better. The unbelievably easy access of voice recording, pictures, and video with which to post to social media made places like these a dry, quiet outpost. A perfect place where she could relax for a couple minutes and truly get a break.

Liz strode in. They acknowledged each other with a smile. Three years ago, they had met when she started at a boutique PR firm in Georgetown. Liz helped her get this job with the Congressman. Madeline wanted an interesting resume, so she said yes when a position was offered, even though it was half the money. Liz went to the counter and ordered her usual drip coffee with room for cream.

"The coffee here isn't bad you know," Liz said as she approached the table. "But I'll be damned if I'm going to spend more than two bucks on one." She hovered near a chair, but didn't sit down.

"I wish I was in Italy right now," said Madeline dreamily, remembering the trip she took with her dad to source grapes for his winery. "Even gas station coffee could beat a place like this."

"Don't we all wish we were in Italy right now? Should we get going? I have the conference room booked so we can discuss the press release."

"Take just a minute and breathe in the delicious aroma of your coffee."

Liz relented and dropped into the chair opposite her. "It's a drip coffee. There is no delicious aroma. What's with you today? Usually you are caffeinated to the hilt and ready to jump off a cliff. Something happen?"

"Actually, I am calm and relaxed. I have a date tonight. Jack. Lawyer. Bingo four." Madeline wanted to appear nonchalant, but was carefully gauging her friend's reaction. Liz could hide her facial expression better than anyone she knew. If that girl wanted to take up professional poker, she'd make a million, ten times over. There was a glimmer of annoyance that crossed her face. The only way Madeline would have seen it was to pay close attention.

"Bingo. You don't think I'm... No. Unequivocally absolutely no." She seemed a bit flustered, a quick glance to the side, a fast bite on the lip.

"You *really* aren't going to play?" asked Madeline.

"No. I'm not interested in the least."

"Okay. Your choice. You know, it would be a little odd, for me, if Cheyenne won. She does work for me. Not technically, I'm not her manager, but still, she reports to me."

Liz looked around them, but no one was within earshot. The place was empty. She leaned into Madeline. "Be careful. Don't tell anyone about this. If someone over the fence finds out, you'll get fired, and that will be the positive aspect. Gretchen, our favorite social blogger, would eat you alive."

Madeline sat up tall, looking around her. She had already run through all the likely scenarios that could happen from playing this game, she was a PR whiz. The worst-case didn't seem likely, and she hedged her bets against anyone of consequence finding out about the game. Hearing Liz talk about BINGO out loud like this brought home just how dangerous the game could be.

Madeline stirred her coffee, watching the swirls of light and dark. Even so, she was in three deep. She couldn't stop now, not when she was on the verge of winning. She didn't want to stop. She already had her Vegas weekend planned out.

"I have a meeting with Eleanor later today. I'm going to introduce her to my dad and see if he's interested in the seating chart program."

"That app was amazing. If I had to do that stupid seating chart by hand, I'd still be locked in my office."

"I thought you two didn't like each other."

"Why? Because we aren't super-duper friends? We work together. She's my colleague and I respect her. And her work is amazing."

"That's true," Madeline said, ignoring the sarcasm. "Now, enough of that and let's get to the point. Let me help you. We can spice up your dating life. Would you like me to create you a page on Tinder? Or Match?"

"Are you serious?" asked Liz. Her jaw clenched up, but she smiled forcibly.

"Yes. I am serious." Madeline ignored the signs to cease and desist. "I have never heard you talk about a guy. Ever. Not even like a date. Either you are extremely private about your dating life, or you have none. I'm going to guess which one it is."

"Playing BINGO is not how you date. You are,

like, obsessed with this game. What has gotten into you?"

"Don't try to change the subject. I am signing you up for a date." Madeline cupped her coffee. Was she obsessed with this game? Was she more like her mom than she was willing to admit?

"Not this week. I have way too much to do. Literally, I am out every single night on official business." Liz took a sip of her coffee, and looked to the side "When do I have time to try to find a date, let alone go on one?"

"I get back from the Hamptons on Sunday afternoon. How about Monday?" She took a drink and sighed. While it wasn't Italian coffee, the barista did a great job. It was delicious.

"If you want to win, you shouldn't be helping me."

"I don't think one date will push me out of the running dear. Next week, I will be setting you up on a date."

"I'm completely inundated with the Chinese visit this week. I just can't."

"You have to try."

"Why are you so intent on getting me to do this? I'm just way too busy with the Chinese delegation this week. Seriously. No. Time." Liz picked up her computer bag.

Madeline didn't try again; Liz's demeanor was like

a steel beam. She could try, but she wouldn't get very far. How had her sister known that Liz wouldn't play? Maybe she wasn't that great at reading people. Nah. It was a fluke, she was good. It wasn't an exact science anyway. "Shall we head to the conference room?"

"Get your bag," said Lizbeth. "And don't try to kiss anyone on the way to our meeting."

Chapter 3

The evening weather was hot and muggy, even with the air conditioning on. Heat-induced sluggishness had her wishing she could just loll on the sofa in her apartment. She was revived by the promise of a fun date and the prospect of getting closer to her BINGO win. She changed into a flower-print miniskirt and a white silk shirt. The outfit paired perfectly with her Jimmy Choo high heel sandals that she had bought during her lunch hour for the Hamptons party. She would wear them on her date to break them in. Besides, comfort was relative—especially with such good-looking shoes as these, even if they did pinch her toes a bit.

She didn't want Jack to pick her up, so they had arranged to meet in the lobby of the Sequoia in Georgetown. If she needed to bail, going to a restaurant with plenty of cabs nearby proved to be a very effective mode of escape. As she waited for him in the world-renowned restaurant, she admired the floor to ceiling glass windows. The Georgetown waterfront provided great people watching. She wondered if she knew anyone with a boat parked on the pier. Wandering along the pier to see who she might run into could be fun, but she dismissed the idea. She needed to spirit Jack directly to The Reflecting Pool for a BINGO kiss—her only objective.

Madeline pulled out her phone to see if he had sent a text. He was five minutes late. A man pushed through the doors with overstated testosterone. He wore a suit just a tad too big in the shoulders, a giant diving watch, and a monolithic class ring on his finger. Madeline rolled her eyes. *Oh no.*

She had been on enough dates to know within the first ten seconds if it would be good or not. This was disappointing—she had liked him so much during their text session after her phone call with Aundrea. *Give him a chance Asher.* Maybe his sense of humor would shine through. If not, well, she'd at least get a BINGO kiss out of it.

He approached her cockily and asked, "Are you Madeline?"

She stood up and glanced at his pin stripe outfit. He had come straight from work without bothering to change. The hostess stood at attention with the menus. Jack held his hand out to her. "Perfect timing."

His smile was over the top, with an air of fake sincerity. *Seriously Asher. Give him a chance.* Even so, she didn't want to take his offered hand, but did anyway, and they followed the waiter to their table.

When they sat, Madeline always put her napkin on her lap immediately. She half-wished she would stop because, eventually, the napkin would slide off her lap and onto the floor before dinner. Jack ordered wine for both of them before she even had a chance to look at the menu to decide what she would eat and if the wine would be paired properly. He ordered a decent wine, a Cabernet from California, but she preferred Meritage. And maybe she wanted white. The point: he didn't even ask.

Likely, he will technically be a good kisser. All the moves, but none of the heart.

Madeline looked away from him and at her lap, but the napkin wasn't there. She bent over to pick it up, shook it out, and placed it back on her lap.

"I was late because a client buzzed me at the last minute. Of course, time is money, so I had to listen to her whine and bitch about how she hates her new house. A 35-million-dollar house mind you, and how the tile isn't right and she wants me to sue the former homeowners so she doesn't have to pay for it. You can't make this shit up. Of course, you know I listen to it because I have to. I'm paid to do it, and it's a favor for my best client, but days like this that make me feel I'm just some hick lawyer ..."

"Your profile says that you do corporate litigation."

"Weren't you listening? It's a favor for a Fortune 500 CEO. His sister-in-law. I tried to suggest another attorney more suited to her needs, but she wanted me."

Dates like this were a solid reminder that she needed a new watch. Perhaps she had stopped wearing them because she was tired of looking at all the time she was wasting. Maybe she could talk Eleanor, the IT guru at work, to develop a program for interrupting dates with automated phone calls. Lots of people asked friends to call them on first dates to check in, but Madeline would love something she could manage without help.

She smiled politely and nodded at him when he paused. He'd take a quick breath and keep talking. Bladdity, bladdity, blah blah blah.

He came up for more air, and she tried to jump into the conversation. "That's so interesting, you know I..."

"Let me finish," Jack said, cutting her off. "I'm in the middle of my story."

Madeline smiled and gritted her teeth. Where was the damn waiter? Maybe Jack would shut up for two minutes so they could at least order dinner. *Fucking asshole.* He better not be so presumptuous as to order for her. Without realizing it, she had finished her glass of wine. A waiter happened to be coming by so she raised her glass to him. He nodded and returned almost immediately with a second glass for her. She let out a brief sigh of relief.

The waiter pulled out his little notebook. Madeline had already looked at the menu and knew what she wanted, shrimp. Sequoia was one of the best places to get seafood in town, and although she loved crab more than shrimp, she had never ordered Blue crab again after having had Alaskan King Crab that her dad ordered special for a dinner at the winery.

"I'll take the house salad with the balsamic vinaigrette to start with and the shrimp special. Thank you."

"Right away, and for you?" asked the waiter, directing his attention to Jack.

Instead of ordering, Jack looked right at Madeline. "Are you sure you want to order the shrimp? The crab is much better."

"I'll stay with the shrimp, but thank you."

Jack crinkled his eyebrows in concern, then turned to the waiter. "She should let me order for her. Obviously, she doesn't know how good the crab is here."

The waiter looked back and forth between the two

and shifted his weight from side to side. He held his pencil above his pad and looked at Madeline with a forced expectancy.

"Just the salad and shrimp for me," Madeline said, smiling at the waiter. She redirected her gaze back to Jack. "You should order. I want to hear the rest of your exciting story."

God, she wanted to leave. The only reason she directed Jack back to his story is so that she wouldn't have to share anything about her. *As if he'd even care.* If she didn't need him to pucker up for a kiss at the Reflecting Pool, she would have excused herself a while ago.

He shrugged and turned to the waiter. "We'll start with the scallops to share. I've got to make sure she doesn't miss out entirely, am I right? And, of course, I'm having the crab. That way she can taste it and know exactly what's she missing." He winked at the waiter as if to say they both knew better than she did.

Before she had a chance to tell the waiter to keep the scallops the hell away from her, she was allergic, he waved away the waiter and continued with his story. "So then, I have this friend who is an investment banker up in New York. He's crazy you know, knows all the designers and models in town, so when I go up to visit him, it's basically dinner and strippers. God Bless America."

Strippers and God Bless America in the same breath? She had to check herself from looking at his neck to see just how red it was. What kind of man admits to visiting strippers on a first date?

"Why not stay in New York? What brings you to DC?"

"Well, my big clients are here. It's easy money. I love New York, but if I lived like that every day it'd give me a coronary. And speaking of coronary's I know this doctor out in Chicago, I can't tell you how much money she makes, but let's just say private jets are no problem, and so..."

She smiled and nodded as he droned on, not really listening to him any longer. When he paused to take a sip of his wine, she excused herself to the bathroom. Madeline didn't actually have to go, instead, she found her waiter and asked him to assure dinner service would be prompt and that she would always have a full wine glass. With the request, she handed him a crisp hundred-dollar bill.

This date was probably the worst one she had ever had. Worse than the commercial developer whose only interest in life it seemed was... developing. Worse than the chef who tried to feel her up like a chicken breast, and worse than the FBI guy who tried to jam his tongue down her throat... frankly, the list could go on and on. Maybe she was at the end of her rope with dating. It used to be fun, but lately, it did not feel worth the effort of even getting dressed for, let alone getting her hopes up.

"About time you came back," Jack said when she sat down. "I was wondering where you got yourself off to."

Madeline only smiled at his response. He probably asked about her welfare only because he had no one to verbal vomit with.

"My dad wanted to have dinner with me tonight, but I opted to share a meal with you instead," he said, grinding his teeth and trying to smile at the same time. The creep factor multiplied exponentially. He would have made a perfectly bad meme.

Declining to engage over his passive aggressive dig, she asked, "Does your dad live here?"

"No. He flew in from Michigan, upper Michigan. When my parents retired, they bought a little cabin out in the woods. He wanted to spend his days fishing." A genuine smile appeared followed by this sweet, almost little-boy laugh. For the first time, she glimpsed the funny guy she'd texted with the day before.

"He flew all the way out here? And you're not having dinner with him?"

Nonplussed, Jack pondered before answering, which was a bit of a surprise in and of itself. He took a drink from his glass of wine, and swirled it, watching the liquid legs slide down, "He's fine on his own tonight. He said he was too tired to go out and wanted to chill, so he's at my place with Netflix." He paused to look at Madeline. "He was a traveling salesman, so I didn't get much time with him."

She knew exactly what that was like. Her parents were busy working their important jobs. Something or someone was always more important. "That must have been hard growing up. Having him gone so much."

"He missed a lot of my baseball games, you know, it's funny how you miss the little things right? I just wanted to like, sit with him, hang out and play video games."

He glanced up and met her eyes. His sweet smile faded and a hardened look came over his face, "But you know, who cares right? It's not that big of a deal." He straightened his silverware on the table. "Enough about that, let's talk about you. What do you think about me?" he said, with a light laugh.

"Oh. Haha." An awkward silence followed, but she was thinking about her own dad. He bought a damn winery to be closer to them in high school. Was she keeping him at arm's length? Why? To make him pay for working so hard when they were young? The waiter appeared magically to fill up both glasses of wine and deliver six elegantly plated scallops.

He slid the plate over to Madeline, offering them to her first.

"I'm allergic. I can't even touch them."

"Well why didn't you say so?" he said, narrowing his eyes at her as he pulled the plate back. "Jeez, you try to be a gentleman...."

He stabbed the first scallop with a fork and put it into his mouth whole.

She bit her lip, holding back her acerbic tongue. She was a master of small talk, so the conversation revolved around the latest movies and TV shows. After the plates were cleared, they skipped dessert. They split the check and walked to the back bar to have a drink and people watch.

It was too crowded, so she suggested they move on to Tony and Joe's, one of her favorite bars. She recognized a few people, and so did he. Introductions flew by. She met one of his coworkers, who happened to be just like him. The evening was going to be a bust if she didn't get a BINGO kiss. She had to kiss Jack—*ugh*—at the Reflecting Pool. That meant they should leave now before the evening took off as a social event.

Madeline approached Jack and stood very close to him. His body radiated heat. She put a hand on his shoulder and leaned in to whisper, a romantic sigh at the end of her request. He responded quickly. Jack handed his beer over to his friend and asked him to pay for the drink. He grabbed her hand, and they walked past the water fountain, lit up beautifully against the night sky. At the cab queue, the manager hailed one and told the driver to head for the Reflecting Pool.

THERE WAS no cab drop off at the Reflecting Pool, so they were dropped off at the Lincoln Memorial and planned to walk to the pool. Tourists buzzed about the site, but quite a few less than during the day. He paid for the cab, then walked around to open the door for her. At least he could act like a gentleman when he put in the effort. He might be an okay guy, maybe, if he wasn't so stressed about impressing her with his name dropping.

The evening was still hot and humid as if they were in a gigantic steam bath; a precursor of summer weather. Kissing him, sure, would keep her right on track to win the game. But what was the point of winning? Sure there was the conference that would change her career, but remnants of Aundrea's conversation drifted in. *Someday it'll just hit you between the eyes.* Wasn't there more to life than trying to scheme for a kiss?

"My dad and I came by here the other day." He swept his hand towards the other monuments. "Sometimes I wish I could give it all up and go back to Minnesota. I'd be a fishing guide," he said, his expression taking on a wistful gaze. "And ice fishing? Oh, man. That's the best." This little glimpse of Jack as a happy man with a look of contentment on his face almost made up for the whole date. Almost, but not quite.

"Let's go that way," said Madeline. They walked around the Lincoln monument and down a dirt pathway that paralleled the pool. Jack pointed out a wooden park bench nestled between two giant Elm trees. *It's just a kiss; it really is no big deal.* Usually she didn't feel so much trepidation over a silly kiss, but tonight, she didn't even want to be here.

Jack didn't waste any time. As soon as they were seated, he put his hand on her thigh, just above the knee and squeezed. Where had the quirky and funny texter gone? It was more than clear what he wanted. What he expected.

But, what did she want?

She closed her eyes to block him out and consider her own needs for a moment. His lips pressed against hers. His hands roved along on her back, pulling her hard against him. She slipped her hands under his jacket running her fingers along his muscles, an automated response. His tongue wanted entry, and she opened her mouth to him, kissing him back, no longer really thinking about what she wanted. Acting out of habit.

Technically he's a five out of ten.

He grabbed at her breast, pushing himself against her. He slid his hand inside her shirt, tugging at her bra strap, trying to force it off her shoulder. "Mmm... yeah," he breathed heavily into her as he broke the kiss.

Relief flooded through her at the break in contact. Clarity smacked her upside the head. This... whatever this was? She did not want it.

She seized his hands to stop his groping. "Jack! Hold on, Jack. Stop for just a second there, big fella."

He leaned back, eyes narrowed on her, breathing hard. "What? What's the matter? Too rough?"

"I just realized that I have a super early meeting tomorrow." The excuse was fast and ready on her tongue.

"Oh. *Right*. I get it. *Let's be friends, right?* You're just like every other broad in DC." He spat the words at her.

"Wait? What?"

"Expect me to pay for dinner and then when it comes to kissy time, you just, you know, you stop."

She'd read him right all along. Self-absorbed jerk. Everything was all about him, and now he was demanding some sort of pay out? She'd seen this before, plenty of times.

"We split the bill, remember?" she said, her calm and professional public relations face on auto-pilot. "I think you should leave."

"Yeah. I'm leaving." He stood up in a huff. "*Women.*" He straightened his tie and jacket. "You know, I am leaving *you*. I am rejecting *you*." He pointed at her with his index finger as if to make himself clear before he stalked off.

Madeline slumped against the wooden slats. *I am leaving you.* Whatever. She pulled her phone out and checked in with Instagram. In spite of the ick factor, she had earned that BINGO mark. She only had one more to go. Could she do it? Could she win? Of course she could. Dating was simply a numbers game, and games were about logic.

She strode off in the opposite direction that Jack had taken off so she could find a cab without having to see him again. On the way, she passed a young couple holding hands and gazing at each other like people in a romance movie. *How do they do it? How did they find each other?* Her fingers tingled with a longing she didn't want to acknowledge. Instead of feeling happy for them, she glared at the couple, but they were oblivious to anyone else.

Chapter 4

Madeline's sister had made arrangements for her to fly up to New York on Bunny's chartered jet. At Dulles, she gave her leather overnight bag to the porter. Soon enough, he returned and led her through a checkpoint and out onto the runway. Her hair blew up and over to the side. She tried to grab it and put it into a ponytail, but it was so loud she chose to cover her ears instead, letting her hair go wild.

Inside the plane, she passed by the white leather couches and opted for a window seat bucket chair that pointed away from the others. She wasn't feeling social and wanted to read up on her latest book obsession about a particularly handsome Scottish highlander. Usually not her thing, she was too pragmatic for romance. Except, there was something about the story that drew her in; maybe it was finding love in unexpected places. The stewardess approached her and gestured for her coat. She took it off and handed it over.

The stewardess returned with a bottle of Krug champagne in her hands. *A nice bottle, a very nice bottle.* It was only four thirty in the afternoon, but what the hell, why not? She wouldn't have to drive from the airport. Her sister had promised to send a driver to collect her at the airport. What a lovely way to end the workday. Champagne and dashing stories of Scottish Highlanders on a private jet. What could be better?

Well, a *real* Scottish Highlander in her life would be pretty amazing. She scoffed out loud. After her date with Jack—a man with the personality of sheet metal and a kiss that matched—Madeline was more sure than ever that sexy, fun romance was for the books.

It didn't happen in real life, at least not in her life. She plugged her headphones in and tuned her music to the classical genre. Before digging into the book, she held her glass of champagne in the air, toasting to no one. "Scottish Highlanders. Hm. Here's to finding one for my very own! Cheers!" This was so silly, but she didn't care. She tilted her glass for an imaginary clink and downed the whole glass.

Madeline stopped reading when the plane entered

the New York City airspace. She could feel the energy from the city, even ten thousand feet up in the air. The Big Apple had a throbbing pulse as if the city itself were a heartbeat, and she had her hand pressed against it. She was glad to be out of DC. Even if the Hampton's party was a total snoozer, which she expected it to be, at least she wouldn't have to be 'on' like she was in DC. She needed a break from work and she was glad to have a break from the BINGO game.

The plane began its descent for La Guardia. Perhaps this party wouldn't be a bore. Maybe Bunny and Skip will have invited handsome Scottish Highlanders to make it interesting. The image of kilts and bagpipes at a Hampton beach party made her laugh. *A girl can dream.*

THE DRIVER STOPPED in front of her sister's place, got out and placed the luggage in front of the entryway. She had forgotten the speed at which New York runs. Groggy from the flight and two glasses of champagne, she thanked the driver and tipped him. Her sister had been unhappy with the real estate choices in New York. She wanted room to grow, so she opted to purchase two side-by-side brownstones. She tore down the separating wall renovating it into a five-bedroom unit. Well, she had her private contractor do the actual work, of course. Aundrea couldn't possibly break a nail wielding a hammer of her own.

Madeline was about to ring the bell when the door opened up straightaway. Aundrea stood there with Ava propped on her hip.

"Welcome sis! I am so glad you're here! Get inside stat!" she said, kissing her on the cheek. "I have missed your face."

Madeline gave her sister a hug and returned the kiss. "I've missed you too, and you, how are you darling?" she said, directing her attention to Ava. "Is your momma treating you well?"

"Can you believe she is already six months old?" Aundrea plucked a stray hair out of her eye. "Oh, my manners. Come in, come in. Dave can't be here for dinner tonight. He's working at the teaching hospital. The nanny isn't here yet, traffic, and I have to pee like crazy."

"You need to be with Auntie, don't you?" Madeline held her arms awkwardly out, not quite sure how to proceed.

Aundrea thrust Ava into her arms before spinning away toward the bathroom.

Ava grabbed a fistful of hair and, twirling it with a bit of force, pulled herself against Madeline's chest. She gently untwined Ava's chubby fingers from her hair. "You're such a big girl. Auntie loves you so much!"

Ava squirmed hard against Madeline. She bounced the baby up and down a little, like she'd seen Aundrea do before, but she continued to squirm. Madeline walked into the living room and gently set her down on a blanket that was spread out with some baby toys and a soft book. Madeline laid on her side next to the baby. Ava smelled wonderful, a new baby smell, with a hint of lavender. Madeline patted her bum, then Ava lifted her head and feet up, like an airplane.

"You're flying. What a good girl!" Madeline said, surprising herself. She wasn't usually this patient with a baby. But, she was calm and relaxed and totally absorbed by her niece. Entranced even. She had never considered herself the maternal type. Becoming a mom had crossed her mind, but in an abstract way, like the idea of going to a faraway land she might visit someday. She wanted to be a mother *someday*. She wanted a family, but she wasn't sure if she'd ever get there. Being with Ava, Madeline recognized a sharp pang of emptiness and a bit of jealousy towards her sister.

Madeline sighed and picked up Ava and patted her on the back. Ava gurgled happily and proceeded to spit up white stuff. It drooled out of her mouth and onto her shoulder, right onto her clean shirt that required dry cleaning. Madeline looked around for something to wipe her with and found a pile of neatly folded cloths on the coffee table. She lightly wiped the drool from her niece's chin and off the blanket. Rather than being disgusted, cleaning and caring for Ava came naturally to her. When she was with Ava, everything seemed to melt in her, she was softer, more easygoing, but she was also tougher; she'd go all momma-bear against anyone who might even think about hurting her.

"That's better," Aundrea said, sauntering into the room. "Emily will be here soon. I gave her the afternoon off since she's covering dinner for us and putting Ava to bed---who is on a new schedule as per the sleeping consultant." she said, checking her watch. "But trains are late. Soon as she gets here, you and I will hit my closet. Sadie, my personal shopper came by with some gorgeous dresses for the party. I made sure to have some of your colors and size brought in too."

Her sister had always been the girly one. She loved dressing up, makeup, skin-care. Madeline preferred a low-key style, her makeup tended to be more on the natural side than the dramatic. Her style of dress was classic; she preferred muted colors to complement her skin tone.

"I told Sadie that you were a spring, with light brown eyes, golden brown hair, and ivory skin with a pink undertone. You look good too. Watching your carbs? Anyway, there will be something perfect for you, I promise." Aundrea dropped gracefully onto the couch opposite of where Madeline sat with the baby so they were facing each other.

Her sister always took good care of Madeline. She was two years older. Their parents were away a lot, working, and Aundrea, well, Andrea always made sure she was okay. Of course, they had argued and had their spats, but Madeline trusted her sister more than she did her own mother.

"How is Mom? I haven't talked to her in a while," asked Madeline.

"I don't know. Belinda is always so busy. I don't know why she doesn't retire with Dad, it can't be about the money."

"When did she cash in her options again?"

"Almost two years ago. She could have easily quit and gone to live with Dad."

"Can you imagine Mom---queen of the city, tech diva of San Francisco---moving out to Napa to live at the winery? What would she do all day? She'd go crazy," Madeline said.

"We've had this conversation. Of course she would have to be in charge, she'd take everything over. That's what would happen. But I'm sure she will never leave the City. How's Dad doing in DC?"

"Great. He got this cute little apartment by the zoo. He's taking a cooking class."

"You're kidding? That sounds fun. Are you going with him?"

"No. But he is testing the recipes on me. We have dinner plans next week, and he's making a Thai dish. Says he's taking the class to be prepared for when he opens up the restaurant."

"If it's anything like his wine, I'm sure it'll be a hit. Oh, oh, oh! Did I tell you? Bunny and Skip were over here about a month ago, and Bunny loved Daddy's wine. She's going to be replacing all the usual with Dad's. Can you believe it?"

"You did tell me, it's one of the reasons I'm here."

"I am telling you again. Baby brain is real." Aundrea picked up a glass of water and took a drink.

"So remind me again, what's the party for?" Ava started to wiggle, so she placed her onto the blanket.

"You're a natural at that you know. As you know, Bunny and Skip are hosting. They just bought a new place in the Hampton's. They're raising money for their foundation Orthopedics Every Family, which helps to bring orthopedic doctors to Central America."

"Sounds interesting. Ice sculpture party or...?"

"One Ice sculpture party, but not two."

Madeline laughed in response. There might not be an actual ice sculpture at the party, but she and

Aundrea had attended so many parties, it was how they rated them. One ice sculpture was a nice party: great food, decent wine, but boring. Two ice sculpture parties were celebrity chef prepared food, great wine, and decorations taken to the hilt. Three ice sculpture parties were usually over the top weddings. Four ice sculpture parties were reserved for those insane parties that bored billionaires had with no expense spared.

"And the more important question, are there going to be any handsome, dashing doctors to flirt with?"

"Of course there will be, what kind of sister do you think I am?"

"The best kind of course."

"From what Dave tells me, there are three eligible bachelors. There are actually four single men that I know of, but one of them is off limits to you. He's a complete dirt-bag from what I've heard."

Madeline was immediately intrigued by the last, of course. A bad boy wasn't afraid of her. He wouldn't treat her like an expensive bauble, or get drunk just to drum up the courage to talk to her. A bad boy was someone who could handle her own tendencies, her intelligence, her own strong character, but a bad boy didn't care about love either.

"Maybe he's a reformed bad boy?"

"Off limits. No. Don't even think about it. I am not introducing him to you, well I might have to, but you are not to like him. There are three perfectly eligible bachelors. Two of them have dark brown hair and one is a blondie. I know you usually don't go for the blondes, but this one is so good on paper."

Madeline raised a single eyebrow at her sister. They were always good on paper. "Oh?"

"He has a Yale law degree and has his own practice in Greenwich. A *very* successful practice I might add."

"That might prove to be difficult. What's the bad boy's name?"

"The bad boy doesn't matter. He is off limits, Mads. I'm not kidding. Now, Corbin does quite a bit of business in DC, at least that's what Dave says, he might be opening another office there. And he has such a great name—Corbin. Isn't that a great name? Maybe you can kiss him at one of the monuments?"

"Aundrea! Don't say that! You didn't tell Dave did you?"

Aundrea shrugged, giving her a wink.

Madeline groaned. She should have known better. Aundrea told Dave *everything*. "Shit. Tell Dave not to tell anyone else, please? You know how small these towns are. The last thing I need is word to get out."

"You'll be fine, don't worry. New York City is *not* a small town."

The front door opened, and the nanny came in

carrying boxes that nearly toppled her. "Here are the packages from the toddler consultant." She placed the items on the couch. "I'm so sorry Mrs. Smythe. The train was delayed nearly an hour."

"That's alright, Emily. You let me know with plenty of time, and I was able to change our dinner reservations. I need to nurse Ava, then she's all yours."

Ava rolled onto her back and made big beautiful googly eyes at Madeline. She scooped her up and handed her to Aundrea. "I'm going to find something to eat while you do that."

"Mi casa es su casa. When I'm finished nursing, you and I are going up to that closet. I made you the macaroni and cheese, but don't eat a lot. There are a ton of carbs, and we are going out to dinner."

Madeline disappeared to the kitchen. She fixed herself a glass of water and dropped a lemon in it. When she took a drink, she didn't realize how parched she was. The cool water refreshed her. She opened up the fridge and took out the homemade mac and cheese. It was her favorite, and she placed a healthy scoop onto her plate. She didn't have to listen to her sister. She'd have a salad at dinner. Besides, a few carbs wouldn't hurt.

Chapter 5

adeline, Dave, and Aundrea pulled up to the 10,000-square foot home decorated in gray weather-beaten cedar shingles with private beachfront in a black sedan. The driver opened the doors. They stepped out and a salty sea breeze caught the edge of her skirt. The driver gave Dave a card which had his cell number to text him when they needed to be picked up.

A staff member greeted them warmly and collected their purses and summer jackets. Aundrea said Bunny and Skip completely overhauled the original 1920 house complete with structural and foundation updates. Madeline wondered which part of the house actually remained, but none of that mattered except the leftover aura and ambiance.

They were escorted to the backyard by someone

from the catering company. In the center of the land-scaped portion of the yard, a white triple-tip tent stood erect flanked by several additional tents. Round paper globes of red, yellow, and white hung from the tents. Small bar tables covered with ivory table cloths were placed strategically around the yard. Each table was surrounded by bamboo chairs with pillow top cushions. The tables were decorated with hand-painted spicy-red candelabras alternated with archi-tecturally interesting orchids. The rest of the yard had dramatic flourishes of heliconias and birds of paradise.

Madeline didn't really want to be to a party in the Hamptons, but she was glad to spend time with her sister. She had been to a hundred parties like it—dry, lots of plastic surgery, and a cadre of professional small talkers. Her parents were part of the high-tech money crowd in San Francisco where lavish, ridiculous affairs were part of the life-style. One man had recreated Mardi Gras on his estate with paid actors.

In her junior year of high school, her Dad sold his stocks and purchased a winery in Napa. Movie stars and chef celebrities flocked to his winery, inviting up friends and hosting garden parties and exclusive tast-ings. Being the daughters of the owner granted them automatic invitations to these over-the-top soirees. After completing her Communications masters from

Berkley, she moved to DC and found a PR job in less than a month. More parties.

Aundrea tapped the back of her arm. When she got Madeline's attention, she pointed to two ice sculptures. Madeline smiled in response. It was a nice party. Very tastefully done. A bit mild in tone. There was certainly no expectation that it'd turn wild, but she knew parties like this, there was always an after-party. She wasn't particularly thrilled to be there, but the location was fabulous, and really, she just wanted to spend time with her sister. She didn't even care if she met any of the three eligible bachelors Aundrea had promised her.

There were a number of people mingling quietly. The catering staff was about, dressed head to toe in black, and carrying trays of hors d'oeuvres or champagne. She wondered if she could guess what type of champagne would fill the glasses and what appetizers they might serve. Given the type of party it was, she imagined the champagne would be Moet, a nice but not expensive choice, and that the hors d'oeuvres would contain buffalo meat or some sort of pecan-crusted cheese, as that seemed to be the latest trend.

She took a glass of champagne, which was served with real crystal, bonus points, and took a sip. Her guess was correct, Moet. As for the appetizers, she was surprised by the mini Cubano sandwiches skewered with pickled vegetables, but she was not surprised by the spicy tiger shrimp. All of this detail told her that this would be a boring fundraising party for the East Coast elite, probably aimed for the mid-thirty to late-fifties crowd. With a shrug, she found a waiter and took another glass of champagne along with another mini Cubano. Madeline searched the crowd for her sister and Dave, keeping an eye out to see if there were any hot guys.

Madeline had on an abstract print dress that the personal shopper had chosen. The skirt fabric was wavy and quite short but for the extended hem of bright coral lace. She was glad to have a skirt on; the evening was cooling down nicely. Madeline opted to wear a square heel since Hampton parties were usually on the grass and a smaller heel was sure to sink straight into the dirt.

"Did you see the hurricane candles? Oh my god. I had forgotten what grown up design feels like. I've been sitting here trying to child proof this party in my head, when in all reality, there are no children here."

"There are definitely no children here, unless you count Dave," said Madeline with a jab at her brother-in-law.

"You better behave," Dave said, returning the friendly tease. "Oh, hey, Madeline, this is Bunny and

Skip. And there's Ewan. Ewan. Come here! He's the one running all the fundraisers."

Aundrea gave Madeline a dark look when the name Ewan was mentioned. Madeline just knew this was the bad boy she was supposed to stay away from. He looked harmless enough. His approach was casual, non-predatory. Well, harmless was the wrong adjective. While he certainly was no Highlander, he was a close *Out of Africa* Robert Redford. As he approached the table, and she got a better look, she changed her opinion. *Damn.* He *was* Robert Redford meets hot Scottish Highlander. He had on a pair of thick rimmed tortoise shell glasses and a seersucker suit. His blond, wavy hair was combed back, not gelled back, like every other stockbroker she knew. *Very good looking.* But well, not her type. She didn't go for the erudite East Coast guy.

"Ewan, I want you to meet my sister-in-law Madeline. She's visiting us from out of town," said Dave.

Ewan smiled. He had nice teeth, straight and white, but not blinding-fake white. It was a real smile too, not one of those lewd *I can't wait to see you naked* grins. There was something adorable about the way the corners of his mouth dimpled. And those gorgeous sea-blue eyes drew her into him.

"Nice to meet you. Hope you're enjoying yourself?"

"The party is lovely." *Lovely. Lovely? That* was what she chose to say? She sounded so boring.

"Aundrea." Ewan said with a cautious tone.

"Ewan." Aundrea's mouth turned into a super-fake smile she plastered on when dealing with odious salesmen.

Madeline was wishing she'd gotten more info on this guy before the party. There was definitely something Aundrea hadn't told her earlier. Whatever it was, it was bad. But when she met Ewan, she didn't understand her sister's zealous attitude. He didn't seem like a creep, and usually, she could tell right away about men.

Dave and Madeline gave each other a quick glance, but neither said anything about the interaction. Aundrea was generally better at hiding her disdain.

"Ewan worked with me in Guatemala. He arrived on the scene, and, to tell you the truth Madeline, I never saw anyone work so hard."

Madeline turned toward Ewan. "So what kind of..."

"That's nice." Aundrea said, cutting her off and scowling at Dave.

He shook his head and mouthed "not now." Ewan looked uncomfortable and glanced towards the bar. Madeline looked back and forth from her sister to Ewan.

"Great," Dave said under his breath. "Ewan, come this way," he said louder. Dave clapped his hand on Ewan's shoulder and redirected him. "I want you to meet some other friends of Bunny's."

Ewan gave Aundrea a nod. It was tentative maybe, but given with no ill will. Madeline was impressed. Before he left, he glanced at Madeline with a different smile, an understated one that promised mischief. She couldn't help but slightly blush and smile back. Ewan. *Huh.* He was good looking, no doubt about that, but nothing was going to happen with Ewan. He lived in New York. She lived in DC. She didn't do long distance, having tried once. In her case, long distance simply provided opportunities for his cheating. The old saying out of sight out of mind was true for a reason.

"No. No. and No. Not him." Aundrea eyeballed Ewan.

"What happened? I've never seen you like this."

"It's not your business. Just don't go anywhere near him."

"Stop treating me like I'm twelve, and tell me."

Aundrea glared back at her sister, "If you wouldn't act like a child then I wouldn't have to treat you like that. All you do is party and play games in DC. Grow up. The world is not always what it seems."

Madeline took a step back. Her eyebrow crinkled

and her mouth dropped just enough to register disbelief. She knew her sister had always been like the parent in the relationship, but she didn't realize the extent that Aundrea still saw her as a child. She didn't want to argue, and unable to come back with a decent repartee, Madeline opted for a change in scenery. All she wanted was space between her and her sister so she could think. "I am going to get another drink. Would you like one?" asked Madeline.

"Dad's Chardonnay. Something light would be nice."

"Sure." On her way to the bar, Madeline scanned the crowd looking for Ewan. She was sure he would tell her the whole story. *Screw you Aundrea. You are not my mom, I'll do what I want.*

MADELINE WALKED UP to the makeshift bar and admired the setup. The catering company had done an amazing job making it look classy with white button-pinch panels and a glossy chandelier lit with tea light candles. She was happy for her dad, getting to be the sole wine source at this exclusive event. His winery business was doing well.

Aundrea mentioned that when Bunny saw pictures of the winery, she said it might be a perfect place to have her niece's wedding. That might be kind of fun---not going to Bunny's niece's wedding---but being a wedding planner at her dad's winery. She did know how to throw a party. And she'd get to be in California with her dad.

It'd be a nice life; she could get out of the constant party scene. Weddings were different than parties. At a wedding, people are happy, love is in the air. There are grandmas and little kids twirling on the dance floor. Parties, on the other hand, were all about seeing the right people and wearing the right clothes. It was a wistful and hazy idea, like a dream or fantasy that didn't seem possible. Besides, if she was honest with herself, she wasn't sure if she could give up the fast-paced lifestyle her position afforded her. It was fun, very fun, even if tiring sometimes.

At the bar, she ordered a Chardonnay for herself and her sister.

"Me. A wedding planner in Napa Valley. Ha. That would never happen," she said aloud to herself.

"I'd marry you," said the guy next to her. "In a heartbeat." He reached over and tried to put his arms around her waist. He was clearly drunk. She wasn't sure how he even got his words out so crisply. He must have a high tolerance. She stepped away from him.

"That's nice of you to say," she said in an even tone. Experience had taught her that the easiest way to get rid of a drunk guy was not an outright no or by engaging with a forced smile, but to simply have a monotonous reply. Bore them away really.

"Damn right it's nice of me to say!" He reached out to touch her arm, and stumbling slightly, ended up grabbing the crook of her elbow. He squeezed hard, and she winced.

After he was upright, she lifted his hand off her and placed it on the bar. Years of fencing in high school and college had given her the muscle strength to push him away.

"Now now little lady," he said slurring. "Name's Corbin. You best remember it when saying our vows." He started to guffaw.

Madeline let out an exasperated sigh. This was the guy Aundrea wanted to set her up with? *No fucking way.* Step two of getting rid of drunk guy. She scanned the crowd looking for a waiter. Usually she could find a way out of a drunkard's attention span when she distracted him with a drink order and another person.

A silky, yet strong voice interrupted them. "Hey there, Corbin."

Madeline turned to find herself staring at Ewan. His hand landed lightly on her hip. The gesture wasn't possessive or flirty, but caring and utilitarian, like plucking a kitten from a tree branch. He pulled her back slowly. They were side by side now. She could smell him, citrus and bergamot. She tried not to look at him, but couldn't help it.

His eyes were targeting Corbin, demanding his attention. "Tell me about the Knicks game."

"Oh man, we had courtside seats you know. I was right there when Rose got the elbow from KP. Dude. That shit was insane!" Corbin sloshed his drink up to his face.

Ewan let her go and stepped between her and Corbin. While she was glad he blocked Corbin for her, she missed the warmth of his hand. Corbin looked at Madeline then back at Ewan and back at her again trying to piece together what had just happened.

"Are you two together?" he asked, his expression unsure of whether to be surprised or disappointed.

Ewan looked at Madeline, not answering Corbin. He winked at her, inviting her to play along.

"Oh fine," she said under her breath.

Corbin had completely missed the interchange between them.

Pretending that some guy was a boyfriend was just about a cardinal sin. She had tried this strategy a few times before, but it always failed miserably. Besides, Ewan was the one who suggested the boyfriend angle, not her. She couldn't ask for a better way to talk to him and find out what was going on between him and her sister.

"You two know each other?" she asked, trying to lighten the mood. "Let me guess how you guys met? Guatemala?" she asked trying to deflect the conversation away from her and back to Ewan and Corbin.

Corbin brushed back his hair. It looked a bit greasy, but hopefully it was just hair product. *Goodness. A lot of hair product.* From what she could see, her sister was way off. Corbin was the one she should be careful of. But Ewan? He handled himself like a gentleman, what could he have possibly done to piss Aundrea off? She had to find out.

"Yeah. I know Ewan." Corbin jerked both hands in front of him, a macho move, a fake start. Ewan didn't flinch. He stepped forward with his hands up, and in front of her, blocking Corbin. *Was there going to be a brawl? In the middle of the day at a tame ol' fundraiser in the Hamptons?*

"We played ball together," Corbin said. "Ewan makes a helluva three point."

"I invited Corbin to come down to Guatemala last spring." Ewan did not look at her when he said this, but kept his stance towards Corbin, protecting her.

"Dude that shot was awesome." Corbin looked at Madeline, then back to Ewan sheepishly. "Dude. I didn't know."

"A gentleman always knows," he said, lowering his hands. "I'm going to help Madeline with her drinks.

Pete's here. He's over there, right by the big tent," he said, pointing to the other side of the party.

"There he is! Man I haven't seen him in ages. See you later Ewan. Helluva forward there too," Corbin said, drunkenly trying to wink at her.

As soon as he left, Madeline directed her full attention to Ewan. "I've got to take this one back to my sister," said Madeline, lifting up the second glass of wine to Ewan and pointing it at him. "And you are coming with me."

As she walked back to the table, she tightened her grip on the glass. Was she really going to flaunt Ewan, right in Aundrea's face? Her heart beat wildly, adrenaline filling her body and making her acutely aware of her surroundings, especially the presence of Ewan. When they got there, Aundrea was nowhere to be found. She had gone to the bathroom.

No one said a word, and Dave looked towards the house where Aundrea was. Madeline decided to use this moment as her opportunity to get away and talk to him—without her sister's disapproving eyes on her. She handed over the glass of wine and told Dave to give it to Aundrea.

"Let's go this way," she said to Ewan, taking his

hand covertly so Dave wouldn't see. Her heart had calmed down, but she was still on edge from the adrenaline in her system. Eager to get away from the purview of her sister, Madeline continued onto the beach where a row of tall sedge grass and a white picket fence concealed the view. It was private with good seating.

She stood at the ungated entrance to the beach and leaned against a whitewashed post. The entryway was a bit breezy and almost chilly. Ewan touched her waist as he walked past and set his glass of wine down on the table. He gathered two beach chairs and placed them next to each other. The wind waved the grass, and the ocean crashed into the sand.

Madeline relaxed into the chair, surprised no one else had come out onto the beach for the sunset. With a long breath, she inhaled the sharp scent of the salty ocean accented with the smell of grass spent in the hot sun. She would have closed her eyes to appreciate the smell if the view was not so inviting. The sky turned shades of crimson and pink layered with soft blue and distant thin clouds of gray. She kicked off her shoes and squished her toes into the soft sand. *East coast beaches were vastly underrated.*

"I met your dad by the way. Well, on the phone. I work as a fundraiser for Bunny and Skip. I gave him the logistics for delivery."

"Oh. Wow. I didn't know that. His place in Napa is wonderful. I love it. It's not my childhood home, but I love it more than that." Usually when she spoke about her dad's winery, she always talked about the location, the exclusive guests and parties, but with Ewan, she didn't feel the need to show off. She didn't want to brag about the cool parties her job in DC naturally afforded her, or to talk in general about anything superfluous. Ewan emanated peace and a quiet strength. Frankly, it was a strange feeling, she was used to men whose energy was faster paced. She herself was used to feeling like she had four cups of coffee, always raring and ready to go, but tonight, she leaned back in her chair and closed her eyes.

Ewan reached over and lightly brushed the back of his fingers against her forearm. Surprised, she glanced over and found him gazing at her with confidence. "So... you from around here?" he asked, his smile changing to a mirthful expression.

"Original," Madeline said with a flirty laugh. "No. My sister lives up here. We're renting a house for the weekend, for the party so she could bring her six-month-old daughter Ava."

"That makes sense. So... where are you from?"

"California. San Francisco, but I spent a few summers in Napa with my dad."

"Is that where you live?"

"No. I'm in DC now. I'm working for Congressman Pierce as his Communications Director."

"Really? I have a place in Arlington. Where do you live?"

At this, Madeline sat up. He was good looking, and even if he wasn't her type, he did live in DC. Who knows, maybe they'd see each other around. "I live in the city, DuPont Circle."

"Maybe we can catch up out there. You look chilly, here take my jacket." Ewan pulled off his seersucker jacket and laid it over her lap, like a blanket. Madeline chuckled in response, surprised at how safe and protected he made her feel. If this was any other party, she'd be mid make-out with some random hottie. She reached into one of his pockets and found a business card.

"Do you need this?"

"Nah. Write your number on the back of one? There's a pen in the jacket."

Madeline found the pen. She pulled up her knees, so she had a place to write and scribbled her number on the back. It was sweet, old-fashioned almost. Usually, she just typed the information right into a phone. She handed him the card.

"How'd you get involved with this charity?" she asked, genuinely curious. She wasn't asking as small talk. She wanted to know what kind of man he was, what he liked to do eight hours out of the day.

"My family knows Bunny and Skip. Two years ago, I had a tough break, and I needed to get out of town. Skip was on his way down to Guatemala and asked me to join him down there." He looked back to the party. "That's where I met Dave. The rest is history."

His expression remained aloof, but Madeline was an expert at reading faces, reading body language had helped her career advance in untold ways. A hint of sadness crossed over his guarded expression.

"Did everything work out?" she asked.

"I suppose. I'm here now, right? Everything in life leads us to where we're supposed to be."

"Waxing philosophic?"

"Sure. Why not? It's true right? I mean, here I am sitting next to you, of all the people in the world." He sat back in his chair and gave her a long look. His blue eyes burned into her hinting of long, slow kisses that take all day.

Her breath quickened, but in an imperceptible way since the ocean breeze rustled her clothing. She wanted nothing more than to kiss him. But he made no movement towards her. She made none towards him. Madeline swallowed carefully. She wasn't expecting to like him, she only wanted to find out why her sister didn't. But he was a man who would not be fooled with physical passion. He was the kind of man who would expect her to be her true self. She could tell he wanted her to be the woman she was meant to be.

Ewan took her hand into his. He placed it palm up and stroked her wrists with equal parts of tenderness and strength. "When I lived in Guatemala, an old woman taught me how to read palms." He lightly traced her hand along a deep curve.

"This is the head line." He cradled her hand in his. "It starts here, between your thumb and index finger. Yours is quite long," he said winking, a finger tracing across her palm. "And... you are intelligent."

She was taken aback. He'd said it in a frank and friendly way. He wasn't joking, nor did he say it in a way that made her feel she should apologize for her intelligence. She leaned towards him, inhaling his unique scent. The smell of soap rose from underneath his muskiness and light-handed cologne.

"It's curved, which means you are realistic, but self-controlled. Good relationship skills. A job in communications?"

A ripple of energy raced down her back. She had already told him that she was the Communications director.

"Yes. You already knew that, though." His gaze stayed steady on her. She wanted to open up to him, tell him everything about herself, to learn everything about him.

"This is your heart line, it's connected to your life line, right here," his thumb caressed the edge of her palm. "There is some worry, some prudence." His thumb traced the line across her palm and down to her wrist. "But mostly you are decisive."

Except love. I'm never sure when it comes to love.

"This is your fate line. It crosses your heart line here," he said, tracing a line from her palm to her middle finger. "I don't know how to read it though." With his thumb, he circled the base of her palm. The light hairs on her arms rose, and the ocean breeze tickled her sensitive skin to goose bumps. He brought her hand against his cleanly shaven face and rubbed the skin against his chin. He turned her palm towards him and kissed her in the place where the heart line crossed fate.

"MADELINE!"

Her sister's scream jolted her, making her yank her hand away from him. Ewan gathered himself and jumped up.

"We're over here," he said, walking towards the gate, waving his hands to attract Aundrea's attention.

"Oh, my god. There you are. You have to come with me. Something's happened to the nanny. She had to go to the hospital. We have to go back, to get Ava."

"Okay. Let's go." Madeline put on Ewan's coat. "I'm going to take this okay, but I'll get it back to you."

"It's fine. Go with your sister. She needs you."

Aundrea glared at Ewan and yanked on her sister's arm. Madeline instinctively jerked right back and pushed her sister's hand away. "Knock it off. I got this. I'm fine."

"Excuse me?" Once the look of shock wore away, Aundrea's mouth turned into a tight line. "Emily dropped a glass jar of baby food and now her foot needs stitches. We need to go." She didn't wait for a response and instead turned tail and stomped away.

Madeline turned back to Ewan. "I'm sorry. I have to go."

"I know." He held up the card with her hand-written information on it. "I'll call."

Madeline nodded and smiled at him. She took one last look at the sunset, flared out with reds and oranges, then swooped down to grab her shoes and hurried up after her sister.

Chapter 6

The South Hampton Hospital emergency room was cold. Madeline was glad to have Ewan's jacket, plus it didn't hurt that it smelled like him. A smell she much preferred over the sterile smell of the hospital. She could still feel his lips on her palm and the way it sent shivers up her arm. On the ride over, her sister did not speak a word to her. Aundrea was beyond pissed. Madeline couldn't understand why. Ewan wasn't anything to be afraid of, unlike Corbin. *Gross.* A decent man beats a good résumé any day. *What did she know about Ewan?* She desperately wanted to ask, but now was obviously not the right time.

When they got to the hospital, Aundrea plopped Ava in her arms, then went into the treatment rooms to see Emily. Apparently, Emily was getting ready to feed

Ava and had warmed up a jar of homemade butternut squash when it slipped out of her hands and crashed on the tiled floor. She was only wearing flip-flops and a piece of splintered glass cut her pretty deep. She called 9-1-1. An ambulance had shown up along with the fire department. A firefighter placed Ava in her car seat and she rode in the fire truck to the hospital.

Thank goodness Ava was safe. Madeline nestled her in closer, her nose nuzzling her soft crown. Her sweet new-baby smell mingled with the spice of Ewan's jacket and the antiseptic of the hospital. It was an odd combination, but somehow soothed her. *She wanted to be a mom.* The sentence popped into her head, and she nearly dropped Ava. A mom? She could barely take care of herself how could she take care of someone else? And besides that, what kind of mom would she be? Like her own mom? Like Rosa? Like her sister? None of the ideas appealed to her.

Ava started to whimper. Madeline's attention came back to her, and she started to bounce her gently. She brought Ava up close and whispered, "Auntie's here sweetness. I love you so much." She did this instinctively. Maybe she could be a good mom. But she'd have to find a suitable father first and these days she couldn't even find a suitable date, let alone a boyfriend, let alone a husband.

Maybe it was her lot in life to be a career woman.

She spent little time around kids anyway. Ava was pretty much it. Most of her co-workers were single women like herself. Kids were an enigma to her. She didn't think of herself as particularly maternal. In junior high, she didn't babysit. In high school, she sat through sex-ed and parenting classes, but never felt an affinity towards motherhood.

When they had the dumb exercise of carrying around a sack of flour like it was a baby, she always left it behind. She almost flunked the class because of it. That video of a real woman giving birth? It continues to inspire her to take her birth control pills with religious zeal. Maybe she wasn't meant to be a mom. With a sigh, she cradled in Ava and inhaled that sweet baby smell. Maybe she was just meant to be the best aunt she could be.

Dave arranged for the driver to take Madeline and Ava home while they stayed with their nanny. Madeline couldn't tell if it was out of a real concern for Emily or not, but she was happy to leave the hospital. Its buzzing fluorescent lighting and antiseptic smell creeped her out, and she didn't like Ava being exposed to all sort of germs.

When they got back to the rental, she put Ava's carrier safely on the kitchen table and tiptoed around the mess on the floor.

"This won't do, we wouldn't want you to get hurt

sweets." Madeline picked up the largest pieces of glass and threw them into the garbage. She used a wet paper-towel to wipe up the food. Just as she finished sweeping the rest of the floor to capture all the tiny fragments of glass, her phone beeped a text notif-ication. It was from Ewan. A sense of comfort washed over her, the same one she'd had when she was with him at the party. It was a nice change of pace, very unlike her normal high-paced energy level.

Ewan: How is everyone at the hospital?

For a moment, it crossed her mind that perhaps she shouldn't text back right away, that she should play the waiting game, but she dismissed the idea as soon as it came into her mind. She didn't have to play any games. He just wanted to know how everyone was, he wasn't trying to be that guy.

Madeline: Great. Emily will live, apparently.

Ewan: Glad to hear it. Talk to you later.

Madeline replied with a smile emoji. She closed her eyes and saw the way he looked at her before taking her hand, the way his eyes held hers. The way his lips against her palm had sent a jolt of something unexpected through her. Her entire body tingled with... what expectation? Excitement? Hope? She'd see him again, at least to give him back his jacket. The anticipation gave her butterflies that fluttered from her belly and into her chest.

Ava was waving her hands and cooing, so Madeline took her out of the car seat and went into the living room. She laid a blanket on the floor and put Ava tummy-down. She sat next to her and leaned against the couch.

"There you are," said Aundrea when she came through the door. She sunk into a nearby chair. "Dave stayed at the hospital to take care of paperwork and talk to Emily."

"How is she?"

"The laceration went pretty deep, but the doctor said as long as she keeps it clean, the wounds will heal quickly. She didn't even need stitches."

"That's good news."

"She used the wrong glass to put the hot baby food in. The glass wasn't tempered and of course shattered when she dropped it. Ugh. She's lucky you know."

"I'm glad she's okay."

"I know this sounds terrible, but the doctor ordered her off her feet for a couple of days, which means I need a backup nanny. Any chance you can stay longer?"

"You're not mad at me?"

"Why would I be? Oh. Ewan. I am mad, but I'm too tired. I still love you. Honey, I mean this. You are not allowed to talk to Ewan. He's not the one. Trust me on this one."

"Okay *Mom*. It's not like we are secretly dating."

"I wish you could stay here. I miss having you around."

"Me too, but I can't. I have two huge projects due this week."

"And your BINGO game to win."

Madeline winced at the mention of BINGO. Being with Ewan had somehow made her forget all about the game. She didn't want to go on a date just to get a kiss to win BINGO, not with him anyway. The game seemed so ridiculous to her, childish, petty, and, well, ridiculous. There was still a pull though, a competitive pull to win no matter the cost. Besides, it's not like her and Ewan were a thing. She had to be a realist, and the BINGO game was real.

"And BINGO," she said with a sigh. Madeline picked up Ava who rewarded her with a tiny burp that was borderline cute. She automatically patted her back.

"You're a natural you know."

"You said that already. Just because I know how to pat a burp out doesn't mean I can raise a child. Besides, I don't even have a boyfriend, let alone husband to procreate with."

"You don't need a husband. Just inseminate yourself and come live with me."

"Right."

"It'll be fun! We can take baby drumming classes together."

"Thank you, but I will have to decline. If I am ever a mom, I want to try without a nanny."

"Is that some kind of dig at me?" asked Aundrea in her classically straightforward manner.

"No. Well. Not at all. If I'm a mom, I want to know if I can do it on my own."

"Sure you can. It's easier with a nanny though. I mean, I never realized until she came how all-encompassing being a mom is. It's fucking hard, and I have it easy."

Madeline had pushed her luck with the nanny comment. Anything further could push Aundrea into linebacker defense mode.

"It really is better with a great husband. Dave has to work crazy hours, but he's pretty awesome as a dad," said Aundrea.

"Yeah, he is. You're lucky you found him. It's harder than you think these days. Not to change the subject, but when is her bedtime?"

"Now." Aundrea swaddled Ava swiftly and precisely into a bite sized baby burrito of cuteness. "You know, I'm not saying this because I'm her mom, but she is a good baby."

"The best." They put Ava down in the upstairs bedroom where they'd set up a pack and play earlier.

Ava settled down easily, and they hovered for a bit, watching her relax into a deeper sleep before tiptoeing out of the room.

Back in the kitchen, Aundrea poured herself and Madeline a glass of water. As they sat at the table, Aundrea put on her serious 'I-have-something-of-great-importance-to-impart-to-my-dear-sweet-little-sister' face. "You really should stay away from Ewan. I've heard terrible things, really awful. I mean, Dave loves him, but the stories about him and the ladies? I've heard other stories—*horrible things* from friends who shared in confidence—things I can't share with anyone, not even Dave. I don't want you to get hurt. I know how sensitive you are under that armor of steel."

So that was what had Aundrea going. *Stories.* Madeline suppressed her annoyance. Aundrea had a couple of close friends, but the way she made it sound, there was a gaggle of women who dumped their woes on her and made her swear a blood oath. *And what about me? Why didn't she just tell me? I told her about BINGO.* "You just praised him and vilified him in the same sentence."

"He isn't good for you Madeline. He always has a woman on his arm. I'm surprised there wasn't one tonight."

"I know you're looking out for me, but I can handle myself. I don't need you to mommy me."

"Mom wasn't there, so I was."

"Fair enough."

Aundrea's face softened. She reached across the table and took Madeline's hands in hers. As always, her sister's touch was soothing and warm. She looked out for her. In a quiet voice, usually reserved for calming Ava, she said, "the truth of it is, I don't want to nurse another one of your broken hearts. They're brutal."

"Yeah," said Madeline quietly. "I don't want another one of those either."

adeline liked private planes mostly because of the leg room. And the free wine. And the fast service. After settling into her seat with an actual glass of a most excellent Syrah, she checked the Instagram accounts for the other girls in the game. Madeline was pretty sure she had this one in the bag. All she needed was one more kiss with a fundraiser at the Carillon.

But could she do it? Did she want to? She pictured Ewan's face, and a sense of peace came over her, and nothing else mattered. It had been the same when sitting next to him watching the sunset in the Hamptons. The whisper of a kiss against her palm had awakened something primal within her. It was such a strong feeling for such a light touch. Reliving the memories of that night with Ewan was harmless enough if not indulgent.

She pushed away thoughts of her sister barking orders to stay away from him. Nothing would probably happen with Ewan anyway. Of course she would win BINGO, and life would go on.

A notification popped up that Ewan had followed her on Instagram. She clicked on it and saw a picture of him holding a toddler in tattered clothing. Ewan had the most adorable dimples. She automatically followed him back, then went to check out his pictures. There were several of him in Guatemala. He was either holding a baby or had his arms around the shoulder of someone in every one of them. How could her sister think so badly of him when it was so clear to Madeline what kind of man he was?

A photo of Ewan as part of a wedding party made her inhale sharply. All the men wore tuxedo jackets with tartan kilts. She clicked on the image to enlarge it. *Holy hell. Those thigh muscles.* She fanned herself and looked around the plane. Fortunately, the three other people on board were as deeply attached to their phones as she was.

After looking at them all and reading the comments, she'd put together a pretty good story. His brother had gotten married in Scotland. She focused on one photo in the batch of twenty or so of the wedding that had to be of Ewan's close family. Ewan stood next to his brother, the groom. They were flanked by an older man that had to be their father and a strong looking woman who might be their mother. There was no resemblance to either Ewan or his brother, so possibly a step-mother. An older somewhat frail woman was sitting in front of the other four and sported Ewan's smile. This had to be Ewan's grandmother—the matriarch.

A few other photos showed Ewan dancing in a group of peers. Another showed him off in a corner with a drink in front of him. His dimples were gone in this photo. He looked more lost than anything. Someone had captured a private moment. It reminded her of the same look that had crossed his face when they were in the Hamptons. The image made Madeline want to pull him into her arms and tell him everything would be okay. The sudden protectiveness startled her.

Madeline closed Instagram, afraid to delve any further into his record. Maybe she'd gone one step too far. But that was ridiculous; she was only looking at pictures. And he had followed her. She turned the app back on and pulled up the image of Ewan in a kilt next to his father and brother. They were only a few years apart and had their arms around each other with big, goofy grins. She focused on it for a minute. That's the image she wanted to keep in her head. Hot man in a kilt.

The plane landed without any great fanfare. She took a cab home. At her apartment, she unpacked and ran a hot bath. She sprinkled in tea-tree and citrus essential oils. The smell vaguely reminded her of Ewan. She slipped into the water, letting the warmth cover her belly. Her hard nipples poked out of the water like lone islands. She imagined Ewan and his intense blue eyes on her. Madeline closed her eyes.

With one hand, she retraced the pattern he had drawn on her palm. A ripple of energy spread down her arm and into her body. She cupped her face gently before kissing her own palm, pretending her lips were his. *Fate and love.* Her hands traveled down her body. Her nipple hardened as she twisted it lightly. With the hand he had kissed, she traveled over the flat of her belly and rested it on her mound. She curled her hips up and she spread herself open with a finger. Warm water cascaded in.

The best kind of indulgent behavior. She slipped her fingers inside, softly at first. But her body didn't want soft. Her hips bucked against her finger, wanting more. Her index finger drummed her clit as if she were at a ceremonial event. Her hips moved to meet the tempo. Water swished back and forth, stimulating her, adding to the growing sensation from insistent fingers.

She started to pant and arched her back as an orgasm exploded through her core. She rode it with practiced ease as the waves rippled through the rest of her body.

She collapsed back into the water. *Whew.* She had orgasmed so quickly just thinking about him; she wondered what it would be like with Ewan actually at the helm.

MADELINE GOT out of the tub and patted herself dry with a fluffy white towel monogrammed with her initials. The phone was ringing so she wrapped the towel around her body and headed for the kitchen.

The name Momma Dearest appeared in black lettering on her smart phone. She considered not picking up just yet; she was just so tired of everyone in her family telling her what to do—Mom wanting her to manage Dad... Aundrea butting her nose in about Ewan. She wasn't a kid anymore. Even so, it was hard to get ahold of Mom. Madeline rolled her eyes and mimicked, 'I'm so important' before she answered.

"Hi Mom. I'm still in a towel, so putting you on speaker phone while I change."

"No problem darling. Have you had a chance to speak with your dad yet? He moved out there last week, and he hasn't called me yet."

Did she sound disappointed or just peevish and entitled?

"I talked to him. He's cooking me dinner tomorrow night."

An Instagram notification flashed on her phone. It was from Cheyenne. She had another BINGO check in with the number 4 in her message. They were now neck and neck. She'd have to scroll through Tinder and Match and set up her fifth date for Monday night.

"Is he really taking a cooking class? That's what I heard from his assistant."

"Yep. International flavors of the world. The title is a bit redundant, but the course is taught by up-and-coming chefs."

"Anyone on Top Chef?"

"Really, Mom. You need to get out more."

"I haven't decided if I like Top Chef better or Iron Chef."

"His cooking class only has James Beard winners."

"Why can't he learn to cook by watching Top Chef? I've been able to."

"I just got back from Aundrea's. Went to a fundraiser up in the Hamptons with her and Dave. Everyone is happy. Doing well."

"How's my baby granddaughter? You know, she looks just like I did when I was a baby. Isn't she the cutest thing?"

"Yes. She is. The fundraiser was okay." She didn't dare tell her about meeting Ewan and the drama with her sister. She could just imagine how all that would totally spin out of control.

"Didn't they want Dad's wine for that?"

"Yes. He donated wine for the event. Any bottles he sold afterward, all proceeds went to Skip's charity."

"When are you coming back to visit me?"

Madeline wasn't surprised by the switch. Rather than add more pleasantries upon pleasantries, she changed the subject. "I've got a huge project coming up in Vegas…" She almost told her mom about BINGO, but held back just in time. "It's a charity event in Sin City that Pierce is attending."

"Vegas is very close to home. You'll have to let me know, I can have the jet pick you up."

"I might, but … I don't know." She'd have to win the BINGO game first. She glanced at the dating app shortcut on her phone, but the idea of scrolling through a list of guys made her a little sick to her stomach. "I may not be able to go. It's up to Pierce." There was no reason to tell her mom the truth about the game. It wouldn't go over well with her, anyway.

"You are the master of your own fate, never forget that darling. Make sure that you are indispensable on the team."

Madeline could swear that she could predict their

conversations with at least a 97.99% accuracy. That percentage bumped up to a hundred when Mom talked business. She had a treasure trove of quotes about positive motivators, a big part of what she said it took to be a successful C-level exec at a tech company in San Francisco. Mom had just paid---or rather the company paid---beaucoup bucks for her and her team of women managers to meet a self-help guru whose latest book would spur them to success. It had made an impact, and she talked nonstop about it.

Easy there Judgey-Mc-Judgerson. The truth was, Madeline did like the idea of self-help, making yourself better, realizing potential. People *should* feel good at their job. It's just that, sometimes her mom was over the top about it.

"We can Skype now that I'm dressed."

"Okay. I miss my baby's face."

"Just so you know, there's no makeup on this baby's face." Even though she had just taken a bath and had no plans to go anywhere, her mother had criticized her way too many times for not putting on her makeup. *Perception is the honey that keeps the bees buzzing* she'd say. *What does that even mean?* Madeline bit her lip, she hadn't meant to blurt out the sarcastic remark, but didn't apologize.

"Like you need any."

That surprised Madeline, Mom didn't usually

compliment her regarding beauty. Smarts, yes. Grades, yes. Job promotions, yes. Beauty, no. *Hmm.* She sat down at her desktop rather than using the Skype app on her phone. That way if the convo got boring, at least she could scroll through her favorite sites on her phone. They both logged into Skype and closed the cell call.

"You look beautiful as always darling. There is a glow coming from you, it's lovely."

"Thanks Mom." Sometimes her mom sounded like an English grand-mum rather than a high-powered CIO.

"Your father is driving me nuts. I want him to move back to San Francisco with me."

"He hasn't lived there in almost a decade. Why are you getting upset now?"

"When he moved to Napa, I thought it would last six months, and then he'd be home. He stayed though, and we made it work. He flies up and we spend a few wonderful days together. Or I'll fly down to Napa and have an amazing weekend. You know I met him in junior high. The thought of not having him in my life is ... Anyway, I've just been busy. He's busy. But it's well past time. I need my husband home."

"You're going to have to keep waiting. He's in DC for a while. You can stay in bed and marathon watch Iron Chef."

"I need a decision; I don't need him here right this minute. Oh bupkis. I am just never happy am I? The house is so cold without your father here. Maybe that's why I'm at work so often."

"What are you talking about? You love the adrenaline you get from work. Besides, Dad is only here for a short time. Why don't you take time off and fly out here?" Madeline held her phone in her hand and hid it under the Skype view so her mom wouldn't see her. She clicked on the Match icon. She only needed one more date. One more kiss and she would win the game. She would be heading to Vegas to be a participant in a meeting that would change her career path. She gritted her teeth and scrolled through.

"Are you kidding me?" The impatience in her mother's voice made her look up quickly. The image of her expression on the monitor looked like a kid caught trying to sneak out of detention. Her mother raised her eyebrows and looked down with pursed lips. "I can't take any time off. We are in the middle of a release! My text messages are blowing up to say nothing of my email. We've done enough of these releases, you'd think we would have mastered them by now, but no, everyone runs around scrambling."

That was the corporate life. Her mom had effectively turned every aspect of herself into a gleaming and vital cog in the wheel. Just like she was doing in her career. "Okay. So, when are you coming out to visit?" Madeline held her smartphone in her lap. She knew the Match page was up, but had not yet looked at it. She wanted to click through the pictures, but she didn't dare while on Skype with her mom. It was a bit hypocritical of her. Of course all *her* interruptions were important.

"I don't know. I have Dad's calendar with me. He left it behind. You know, he likes to handwrite everything these days rather than just using his smartphone. It's a pain really, I can't coordinate with him easily. We have to actually discuss our schedules. I need to send it to him, and I don't have his new address and I can't get ahold of him on the phone. Would you be a dear?"

"Mail it to me. I'll make sure to get it to him."

"I don't know about his new assistant. He's getting a virtual one. Louis mentioned he was thinking about going without one. Can you imagine?"

"Lots of people are able to manage."

"But he's had Sally since the '90's. And I'll be damned if I'm going to end up taking care of his schedule."

"Mom. Relax. I'm sure he'll be fine."

"He's the absent-minded professor."

"He's a grown man. Stop. Refocus. DC. When are you coming?"

"Oh, alright. I have a client in Tyson's Corner. I

could come in about a month, after the release. Then I'll head up to New York to see Aundrea. Maybe you and Dad could join me in New York too? Have a family reunion of sorts?"

"I can take a few days off when you're here, but I'm not sure I can head up to New York, too. I'll know in a few weeks." She just wasn't sure exactly how her month would play out. Most of the time, she was well-planned six weeks in advance, but she didn't know if she'd be going to Vegas. There was something else though, she wasn't quite sure why, but somehow, she knew her life was about to unravel.

As soon as she hung up the phone, Madeline scrolled through her latest Match mates. She happened to land on a page of a man who was dreamboat gorgeous. He was also a fundraiser, just what she needed for her next BINGO.

Her mouth formed a small 'o.' *Ewan is a fundraiser*. Well, she knew he was a fundraiser, but she hadn't considered kissing him for BINGO. If she closed her eyes, she could almost hear the ocean waves crashing against the sand, feel the way his lips had grazed against her palm. That had been a magical moment. She shook off the idea. There was no way she'd ever play BINGO with him. Ewan was too special.

Madeline opened the Match page again. While

the moment with Ewan had been near magic, that's all it had been. Right? A moment. She didn't believe in true love, let alone love at first sight. She couldn't get her hopes up for Ewan. It wouldn't work out with him long-term anyway. Especially if her sister had anything to do with it, for whatever travesty he had done. She needed to deal with known quantities, and with that, she emailed the Match guy with plans to win this BINGO game once and for all to advance her career—which was more important than daydreaming over a fantasy in a kilt.

Chapter 8

Madeline clipped her way down the hall of the Cannon building and wondered what it would be like to be a woman in this building in 1908 when it was built. Would she have even been allowed inside? She walked proudly through the halls, the tapping of her heels adding to a percussive chorus as other women did the same. The variety of cell phones and text notifications added a musical counterpoint to their shoes. The rhythm of the building must have been so different a hundred years ago.

In the conference room, Madeline expected Eleanor to be there. She was usually the early bird, but not today. Madeline straightened out the thin belt on her sailor inspired pants. She set up her computer with plans to use the extra time to check emails and reply to the ones which could be resolved immediately. The door burst open and Eleanor lurched into the conference room. Everything about her looked normal, her short hair was in place, her clothing snappy, but she seemed harried, as if things were barely in her control, and that was not like her at all. She had never seen her feathers ruffled. Never.

"Are you okay?"

Eleanor turned to her and shushed her, pointing to the little Bluetooth in her ear. "Okay. I've got it. I got it...okay. Thanks. I'll talk to you later." She rolled her eyes and collapsed into the seat across from Madeline.

"What was that all about?"

"People who don't do their job."

"I'm here for you El. What can I do?"

"Nothing you can do. It's IT stuff. Brandon and Sandeep were supposed to have the server issue fixed, but instead ... they don't. And I can't get into this site blah blah blah."

"Blah blah blah? Eleanor. You are always precise. What is wrong?"

"I ...," she looked up from her phone and met Madeline's gaze. "It's nothing. Really. I'll figure it out. I met your dad and Jay, a developer, yesterday. He's really a great guy."

"Yeah, he is pretty great. Good news?"

"We'll see. So far, he's interested in developing it and he wants me to help with his charity app."

"Great news. I hope it works out. And how is the research angle for SUNFLOWER? Is there any chatter? I want to make sure it's kept under wraps."

"It's quiet as a mouse. None of the lobbyist blogs have picked up on it. Twitter is quiet. It's not anywhere. I also ran a check on industry related blogs and events in Vegas. Nothing."

"Kat asked for the PR firm to run an info-sweep too. I can go back to her with solid information, thanks. That reminds me, can you get me everything that's on the webs for two firms: Ellis and Levin Associates and CGF?"

"Yeah. Sure." Eleanor fell back against her seat and closed her eyes, as if the simple request was overwhelming. This wasn't like her at all.

"What is going on?" asked Madeline, studying Eleanor intently. "Something is not right."

Eleanor didn't answer her right away. She opened her mouth as if to speak but closed it again, pretending to look at her phone. Madeline could tell she was buying some time. Finally, Eleanor smiled one of those blissful smiles women usually reserved for a good date or a promotion. She sat up and thrust her shoulders back, shifting her expression into something more of a let's-get-to-it mode. "Ellis and Levin Associates along with CGF? Both are lobbyist firms right? Is Ellis the one Gordy works for?"

"Yes, yes, and yes," said Madeline as she tried to set aside the uneasy feeling she had about Eleanor's behavior. She was not a person who smiled and usually had a serious countenance no matter what her internal emotion. "Remember Gordy works for Ellis and Levin. I want to make sure nothing popped up with Chloe and SUNFLOWER. CGF is related to the hearing that's going on. We have the background, but Kat needs to know if anything else is out there."

"I'll have it by end of day. Do you need it sooner?"

"If you can. Is there something else you want to talk about? I've never seen you like this in the time I've known you."

A flicker of joy crossed over Eleanor's face, but was replaced with a wary set to her gaze. "Just you know, it's the job. Everything seems to be happening. At once. Like always."

Madeline shrugged her shoulders. "You seem happy anyway."

"I do?"

"Sort of. Aside from the IT stuff, you actually smiled. Anything special going on?"

"No. I mean, not really." Eleanor didn't usually waffle, but Madeline didn't want to interrogate her. If she wanted to tell her, she'd tell her. Madeline reviewed the online calendar and saw that Eleanor had a tentative time-slot marked lunch at the Washington Monument.

She lowered her voice to be conspiratorial. "The calendar shows you having lunch at the Washington Monument. You have plans to maybe give someone a quick kiss there?"

Eleanor's jaw dropped open and her eyes widened. "I forgot to delete that."

"Why put it on the group calendar to begin with if you weren't trying to play?"

Her surprised expression turned into an intent focus. "Don't go there Madeline. This BINGO game will get us in trouble. If anyone finds out...."

Madeline looked away and twirled her pen in hand. She had suggested the game never thinking anyone would actually say yes, and her intentions with the game were harmless, to add some fun to an otherwise predictable selection process. The truth was, the BINGO game could be lethal for their careers.

"It's almost over anyway," said Madeline, trying to soften the blow. "I am about to win, you know that, right?"

"Don't be so sure about that, I have my own plan."

"Really now?" asked Madeline, surprised that Eleanor would admit to this. "Care to share?"

Eleanor pursed her lips together, obviously

unwilling to elaborate. "How is your sister, anyway? Didn't you spend the weekend in New York?"

"We went to a party in the Hampton's. I met this guy Ewan. He seems pretty nice." Madeline shrugged as if to dismiss the entire event as completely unimportant.

"And?"

"Well, my sister doesn't want me to see him. I can't for the life of me figure out why though, he is sweet."

"Does your sister's opinion matter that much? Are you going to see him again?"

"It got rather chilly on the beach, so he gave me his jacket to wear. I have to get it back."

"Text him. I mean, if you have his number. And well, your sister... isn't she bossy anyway?"

"She told me to stay away from him. Says he's a lady's man."

"Would you take him to a monument for the game?"

"No." Madeline was a little surprised at how automatic and unequivocal she sounded.

Eleanor pulled back and her eyebrows shot up. "No? You won't play BINGO with him? This is serious."

"Well, I mean, there are plenty of other guys to kiss. I've got a date on Thursday for my final kiss."

"Maybe he should be wary of you?"

"Thanks Eleanor. Am I the femme fatale now?"

"Why don't you get a date and kiss someone tonight? It'd be easy for you."

Was Eleanor trying to be snarky? Or was she genuinely interested? It was hard to read her. "I have dinner with my dad tonight, a PRSA meeting on Tuesday, and meeting my friend Jeannie on Wednesday to celebrate her new job. So, you know, Thursday it is. For the win."

"What if we tie? What happens then?"

"I'm sure we won't. Pretty sure I'm going to win." She'd have to make sure her Thursday date was switched to a lunch date.

"You sure you want to keep playing this game?"

"Course I do. Don't worry Eleanor. I'll let you know how Vegas turns out."

Eleanor didn't look like she quite believed Madeline. "Alright," she said, "I've got another meeting coming up ... are we finished? I could use the time to answer email."

"Yep. We're done. And Thursday for the win." Madeline shot Eleanor a look of bold confidence.

"Go get'em Madeline. I've got to do real work here."

"Real work? We're a team, remember? We help each other. I'll shoot you an email with updates."

MADELINE DEPARTED the conference room as Eleanor stared after her. She walked with steady determination, as if she knew exactly what she was doing, but as she got closer to the office, she slowed down. She checked her smartphone and had no new notifications. Ewan had not yet called or texted since the hospital. Her pace was measured, not quite unsure, but not her usual firmness of step. It took her twice as long to get back to her desk than it usually did.

She buried herself in her email and focused on work.

"There you are. I was hoping I'd get a chance to talk to you." The Honorable Lincoln Pierce had snuck up on her. She was glad she had work open on her computer and not Instagram. "What kind of optics do we have for the conclusion of the SUNFLOWER meeting?"

"Sir, I've written a press release. I will update it as the specifics change so we can hit send within minutes."

"Great news, Madeline," he said with his award-winning smile that won him the cover of Washingtonian as most eligible bachelor. "I appreciate all your work on this."

Opal hovered next to him with a stack of folders in her arms.

"Are all the contacts in place?" asked Opal.

"I have a comprehensive spreadsheet with social media, blogs, and national media sources ready to go. I just finished updating it and was about to email it to you for review."

"What for? Don't you already have a targeted plan in mind?" asked Opal, pushing up her too large glasses and adjusting them.

"That's just it. I wanted to discuss the different options of which media outlets get the first break. I ranked each outlet on the spreadsheet, but figured you might have some thoughts on it. We could send out the release in staggered waves, but how we do it will steer the whole conversation."

"You're right, Madeline," said Pierce. "Opal, set up an hour to go over the particulars. We'll need to get this figured out before we leave for Vegas. Any updates on who is accompanying me?"

Madeline looked to Opal, who was shaking her head in quick bursts. Madeline almost rolled her eyes. Of course she wasn't going to say anything about the game and let out a short grunt.

"Something wrong ladies?"

"No, nothing is wrong, sir," Opal said.

"We won't know who is going to Vegas until Friday sir," Madeline said.

"I'll send you a meeting invite so we can discuss the contact list." Opal made a note in her steno book and checked her watch. "Sir. You've got a Congressional Budget meeting coming up in ten minutes."

Pierce checked his watch and shook his head. "Right. I'll leave you to it then. Opal, I'll see you in five." He turned away and disappeared into his office.

Opal leaned in close. "It looks like you are probably going to win. Pretty convenient don't you think?"

"What are you talking about?"

"Don't play coy with me. You know what I'm talking about, Madeline. This game better not fuck anything up. You know he's planning a presidential run."

"It's not going to. We've covered all our tracks."

"Make sure of it. Because he won't pay for it," she said, narrowing her eyes at Madeline.

"Thanks for the reminder, Opal. I'll make sure of it. I've got work to do." She pointedly returned her attention to her computer. Opal was like a stalking tiger when it came to the Congressman. To avoid confrontation, it was best to avoid eye contact.

She opened her email and read one regarding the date she had coming up on Thursday for the win. With a quick glance, she looked to see if Opal was still there. She was already across the office talking to Chloe. She breathed a sigh of relief.

Now, get back on track Asher. She was tied with Cheyenne and if her assistant got a kiss between now and Thursday, it would be game over. And who knew what was up with Eleanor. She'd been behaving so weird. Maybe she had something up her sleeve. Maybe instead of going to her PRSA meeting, she should go on a date and secure the win. It was in Arlington and her last kiss needed to take place at the Netherlands Carillon, which wasn't far. She could probably meet a random fundraiser in the bar.

Do you hear yourself? What is wrong with you?

Work would help clear her mind, so she dove into writing up the rough draft press release needed for Kat's hearing. She fiddled with it for a while and wrote up two versions. She doubted the hearing would go the wrong way, but she wanted a solid response to it if it did. Just as she was hitting the zone, her phone vibrated, and she jumped in her seat. She glanced around to see if anyone had noticed. It was an unidentified number.

Since she worked in PR, she had to answer the phone. She didn't have the luxury of sending it to voice mail. She tapped on her Bluetooth to answer.

"Hey Madeline. It's me, Ewan."

"Hey, Ewan. Hold on, I'm going to add you." She

had forgotten to put his phone number into her contacts. She scrolled back through her texts. While she clicked an icon to add him, the warnings from her sister crossed her mind. She ignored them. Aundrea didn't know Ewan like she did. The pictures of him in Guatemala were proof of his goodness. So far Ewan was the complete opposite of every jerky guy she had ever dated.

Maybe that's how he gets you.

"How's everything going?"

I am being ridiculous.

"Are you available this week? I'd like to see you."

She could hear the happiness in his voice, he was genuinely excited to talk to her.

"You're in Arlington, right? I'll be in Arlington at the Clarendon Grill Wednesday evening. I'm going to the PRSA's monthly happy hour, but I'm free after, around 8ish maybe 8:30."

"Sure. I live nearby, so it'll be easy to get to."

He continued the conversation asking about the nanny and her flight home. She got the feeling that he wanted to look after her, make sure she was safe. He reminded her to bring his jacket. She wanted to keep talking, but they had no reason once the date was set. After she disconnected, she rubbed the back of her neck.

Should she cancel her date for Thursday? Probably not. Relationships just did not work out for her. Ewan would never work out. She was better off with a known quantity like sex than she was with something she couldn't control ... something like love. And besides, Ewan was probably the guy that her sister described, not the guy she was wishing he was.

Why was it that she couldn't bring herself to just take Ewan to the Carillon for a BINGO kiss? If it wasn't going to work out anyway there wouldn't be any harm in kissing him for the sake of her career.

The very thought of it made her recoil again. How was it that she was worried about tainting him with the game? It wasn't like her to worry about using some random guy she'd just met. There was something about him, though, something that she could not ignore.

Argh! Turn off the analytics Asher.

And what was the story about Ewan that was so damning? Why wouldn't her sister tell her? Aundrea had flat out banned her from seeing Ewan. She wasn't some pre-teen twit. The hell with her sister. Madeline was going to see Ewan.

On the Metro, Madeline flipped through a fashion magazine only half glancing at pictures of the latest trends. She looked forward to having dinner with her dad. They had not seen each other in almost three months, an Easter celebration in Napa. Her sister and her family had flown out that weekend, and mother had been there as well. Dad had a big event organized, mostly for Ava, complete with egg rolling contest for the kids and wine tasting for the adults. The reunion was the first time they had all been together in over a year.

It was a sunny day, but not too humid so she walked the rest of the way to his apartment. In the Hampton's, Ewan had asked her to pass along a verbal thank you for donating the wine. Her dad knew Ewan. Maybe she could get information from him. They only had the one professional interaction. She doubted he had any personal information about him, but anything was better than nothing.

Her dad buzzed her up to his apartment. When she got there, the door was propped open an inch. The apartment was designed with a minimalistic open floor plan. Even though it was a corporate rental, he had taken down the provided stock art and hung up collage pictures of the family. Madeline and Aundrea when they were three and five, dressed up in princess outfits. Madeline in her fencing outfit. Aundrea graduating high school. Belinda actually looking happy while making pancakes. Madeline and Aundrea in the backseat during a road trip, making faces. She didn't realize he had this and wanted to hug her dad and give him a big kiss on the cheek.

She made a mental note to get a copy of the pictures for herself. Mom didn't have pictures like this; all her pictures were ones taken by a professional. Everyone's hair was perfectly done, the four of them in matching clothes and the background always beatific. The style Mom chose lacked any of their personality. They may as well be pre-fab pictures from a purchased frame.

A rich garlicky peanut smell drew Madeline toward the kitchen. Dad had already started cooking. White and gray subway tiles decorated the backsplash, ornate molding surrounded windows and doors, and granite countertops acted as a garnish. The view was nice. The tree tops of a local park mingled with the blue sky. Neighboring buildings were strategically hidden from view.

Madeline's dad looked like a giant in the kitchen. Louis Asher was 6'3 and had played football for Berkeley.

He grinned at her as she entered. "Heya, Honey. This will be the first time I've ever cooked Pad Thai you know. I'm adding shrimp. The chef tells me chicken in Pad Thai is a travesty."

"I think it's the first time you've ever cooked. I haven't even seen you butter toast."

"Come on now, give your old man a break. I made you a mean hot dog once. And mac and cheese a couple of times, too. Kids these days, so ungrateful." He pretended to be upset but cracked a smile.

Madeline returned his expression with a natural laugh. "Dad. I was fourteen, and you used the microwave."

"Humble beginnings dear, don't begrudge a man for trying." He paused and poured her a glass of white wine. "You should take this class with me. It's fun. The chefs are amazing. I mean, how often do you learn from winners of the James Beard Foundation? There's one woman who was a finalist on Top Chef. Amazing class really."

"Mom would love the Top Chef one. Why did they teach you Pad Thai? Anyone can do that."

"Speak for yourself honey. Pad Thai is a subtle but complex dish with spunky fish sauce."

"Funny, Dad. Why are you doing Thai food? The winery looks like an Italian villa, not a fishing village. Shouldn't you match the food to the ambiance?"

"First of all, this class teaches more than Thai. There is Indian, American, Thai, Mexican, and Chinese. Anyway, every other place in the Valley does Italian. I wanted to experiment and try something different. The chef I hire, well, I'm going for fusion."

"Italian-Thai fusion? Like spaghetti with fish sauce?"

"Maybe not that kind of fusion. We'll see. But for now, I am researching with my palate."

"And I will gladly help you do that." Their relationship had always been light and fun. She didn't know how to talk to him about things that mattered to her, and she'd never asked him for advice—well not dating advice. She smiled at him wistfully wishing that she could have a better relationship with him. One that had a little more substance.

Soft music played in the background. He cracked

the eggs and threw them into his wok. They sizzled as he stirred.

"Do you think Mom will like the restaurant?"

"It's hard to tell what *she* will like," he said, the sarcasm was heavy this time. He looked up quickly. "Sorry, I shouldn't do that around you."

"It's okay. Just, well, is she ever going to move to Napa?"

"I don't know. She has the same question for me. Says I should quit this middle-age crisis nonsense, sell the winery and move back to San Francisco."

"When do you get to see each other?"

"Not as often as I'd like. You know, when we were young, we both zipped right up the corporate ladder. It was like we were daring each other to do better. Then, I just got tired of it."

"The corporate life?"

"Yeah, that and the competition with Belinda didn't seem to quit. We were fighting a lot. I was ready to get a divorce, but I thought maybe buying the villa would save our marriage."

"By spending less time together?" Where did this conversation come from? They were deviating from the usual small talk. *Careful what you wish for, Asher.*

"I guess in hindsight it doesn't look that way. It worked well in the beginning. We got to see each other every weekend, kinda had a Disneyland effect, but then we got busy and missed a few here and there. Then more. The subject never came up because we were just so busy. We still love each other. That's not the problem."

"I was sixteen when you moved. Granted, I had a lot going on, but you spent more time with Aundrea and me. Made it to almost every event after that."

"I'm so glad I did it. I'll never forget your senior year duel, that was incredible!"

When he quit his job, he spent more time with them both. It was as though she didn't know her dad all the years before the winery. He was just a ghost in the house. She'd see him at breakfast, sometimes she'd see him at night, but his nose was always buried in his Blackberry.

After he bought the winery, he was a different man altogether. He called to talk to them in San Francisco. He came to all of Aundrea's games. He flew up just to attend her fencing events. In response, Madeline had acted like a bratty teenager or ignored him. She wanted to get back at him for being gone during her earlier years—she wanted to make him pay. But he never gave up. He kept coming to the events.

Over time, she relented, but not completely. The relationship changed to a friendship instead of a parental one, but in some ways, she had never really forgiven him for those absent years. *Hadn't he paid enough?* With a sigh, she glanced back to the pictures of them as a family, hanging in the hallway. They seemed so happy in the pictures.

"I don't know." His voice brought her back to the kitchen. "I don't see your mom much. I mean, what's the point of being married?" He turned his back to the kitchen sink and rinsed off the vegetables.

Madeline picked up her wine glass and swirled it. *Was he talking serious divorce?* As a kid, it terrified her that they would want to split. But as a grown woman, she understood that her parents' lives were maintained outside of her own. People change. Situations change. If her parents wanted a divorce that would be fine. That was the logical way to talk about it, but the topic still scared her --- she felt twelve years old instead of twenty-seven. But was her dad asking her if it was okay?

"Are you telling me or trying to ask me for permission?" she asked bravely. She wanted to know.

Louis turned quite suddenly. "Am I what? Asking for your permission? Wow." He sat on a nearby stool and took a drink of his wine. "Maybe I should switch to whiskey if we're going to have that conversation."

"Let's change the subject then." She swallowed around the tightness in her throat. "Do you need more wine?"

She was about to grab the bottle, but he placed his hand gently over her wrist.

"I didn't realize it came off sounding like that. I wouldn't put that kind of burden on you." He shook his head, his eyes imploring her for understanding.

"It's really okay," she said, pulling away from his touch. She uncorked the bottle and refilled his glass.

"I don't need you to take care of me dear, no matter what your mom tells you."

"Jesus Dad, you know her so well."

"I do." He finished stirring up the shrimp and poured them into a bowl containing the noodles, fish sauce, sprouts, peanuts and eggs. With a sure hand, he tossed the mixture until it was uniform and spooned some onto plates.

"You know the old barn on the back ten?"

Madeline nodded in response.

"I'm having it rebuilt. The plan is to rent it out for weddings. Should be ready in about six months' time, but knowing construction, it'll probably be more like a year."

"What's the plan?"

"We're rebuilding the foundation and then reusing the original boards, or at least the ones that make it. It'll be a quaint red with wooden floor boards. And I'll need a wedding planner. You'd be perfect."

Madeline squinted at him. "Come on Dad. I've got

a full-blown career here," she said, resisting the urge to tell him that she had considered the same career change herself just a few days ago. "Speaking of business, I want to ask you a question. It's about Ewan."

"You're going to ask me about a man? That's a first." He picked up both plates and carried them to the table. Madeline followed with the bottle of wine and set it between them.

"This is business. There's an event coming up, and I was thinking about recommending Ewan for the position." Madeline scratched her neck, just under the ear. It wasn't a total lie, she did know of an open position for a fundraiser at one of the non-profits.

"Is he looking for a job? I thought he was doing well with the Orthopedics Foundation."

"Well. He is, but, well, I want to know what you think of him? Should I recommend him?" She picked up her fork and held it mid-air.

"What is it sweetie? This isn't about work, is it?"

Madeline could feel the warmness of a blush on her cheeks. "It's nothing. Just what did you think of him professionally?"

"I see." He raised an eyebrow in a knowing way and took a bite of his food before responding. He closed his eyes and looked heaven-ward. "Oh. I did good."

Madeline twirled her fork in the food. "I met him

at the Hampton's, with Aundrea. I don't even know him all that well, but, …"

"I know of Ewan. I haven't met him, but I spoke on the phone with him. He called me to straighten out the logistics and financial information related to the donated wine."

"Oh right." Part of her was annoyed. She wanted to skip the lying bullshit and ask him what kind of man Ewan was. She wanted to know if she should trust her gut and believe that he was a good man, or should she trust her sister's advice?

That was the kernel of it. That was why it bothered her—she didn't trust love. All she had gotten for believing in love was bad breakups and dating assholes. But she trusted her sister. Meeting Ewan made her feel backwards. She wanted to find love again. She wanted to trust him in spite of her sister's advice.

"The guy isn't a used car salesman. I hate to say it that way, but anyway, when I spoke to him, he was genuine. A real nice guy. He's smart. Good with numbers. I'd hire him. What does your gut tell you?"

Madeline smiled at him. He always had a way of getting to the real question she wanted to ask. "That he's a good guy." Maybe it was that simple. He was a nice guy. He was smart. And that was all. She wasn't handing over her heart. She wasn't going to marry him for the love of God. She was simply meeting him to give his jacket back. Meeting Ewan wasn't going to change her whole life. That was so melodramatic. She ate a bite of the Pad Thai. "You're right. This is amazing. Better than any restaurant in town."

"I love you honey. Offer's still open, if you want to come out to Napa and be the wedding planner."

"I love you too, Daddy. Thanks for the offer, but I like my job," she said, trying to put her heart into it.

"It was worth a shot, anyway. Don't forget sweetheart, go with your gut."

"Okay. I promise. I'll go with my gut."

Chapter 10

Tuesday morning was the same as any other day. General traffic was still crowded, but with less angst, as if springtime relaxed everyone. The congressional building was old and needed repair. Rain had leaked in over the spring and the drywall in the hallway was peeling. Thank God renovations were started, but they came with their own set of headaches. Madeline entered the office and sat down at her desk, firing up her computer.

"It's almost 9 am. What took you so long?" Kat asked. She hadn't even seen Katherine across the room. How she had missed her, she wasn't sure because Katherine was steaming mad. She could practically feel flames radiating from her body.

Madeline winced. The words were like knives stabbing into her. "The Metro was packed. I thought I had time. Did Chloe forget to send me a meeting invite?"

"No. You're on time, I suppose. I saw your schedule was clear. We need to talk."

"Let me unpack first, and I'll be right with you. Time to get a coffee?"

"Make it fast. Grab a coffee if you must, drip from the office, not the café. I'm on my way to the conference room. Meet me there." Katherine grabbed her leather computer bag from the table. "Five minutes."

Madeline found her go-cup and filled it with coffee. It tasted burnt, so she added a mini cup of fake dairy. She took a moment to gather herself before rushing to the conference room. What could Katherine possibly want? All her work had been on-time, if not raised to a high standard.

Madeline barely made it inside the conference room before Katherine rounded on her.

"Carleen knows about the BINGO game."

Madeline's throat constricted a little bit. When Link was out of the office, Carleen was the boss. Link didn't do anything without consulting her. "What? Are you kidding me? How did she find out?"

How could Carleen could have found out about the game? Did she overhear someone talking about it? They'd all been so careful. And, they'd all sworn themselves to secrecy.

"I told her. She asked me a direct question, and I had to tell her. She had already figured it out on her own, she just didn't have specifics."

"I had forgotten she was at the Capital Bar happy hour, well, not with us, she was having a drink with that intern."

"Carleen knows. You can still play the game as long as you keep it discreet. You know what will happen if this gets out."

Madeline did know what would happen. Even if there was only a rumor that the girls in Congressman Pierce's office were playing a Kissing BINGO game, all hell would break loose. It wouldn't look good on social media, or frankly, any news channel. Gretchen, the premier social blogger in DC, would have a field day.

She'd be fired. She'd have a tough time getting any PR job in the city. No one would find out on her end. Her sister knew, but who else would she tell? Besides Dave. No one had real proof. All they had was circumstantial, "he said-she said" stories. It wouldn't matter though as she imagined the ire and outrage of the pundits on TV.

"So are we quitting the game?"

"We? You need to make your own decision. I am, however, done. You've deleted all the paper copies of the BINGO cards? And you threw out your card? Does the print shop have copies of the game?"

"No. We have a standard procedure that they destroy any digital copies they get from me and they are under contract to not divulge information."

"They are under contract for government materials. I'm pretty sure they won't think a BINGO card is work-related."

"I told him that we created a role-playing game to help our team work better together."

"That was quick thinking. So, there is no external evidence out there?"

"Unless someone figures it out on Instagram. Otherwise, nothing. You've talked to the other girls about their physical cards right?" Madeline asked.

"Not all of them yet."

"Do you want me to speak to the rest of the staff?"

"No. I'll talk to them. You have caused enough trouble with this game," Katherine said, half laughing. "Though, I have to admit, it's not as crazy as other games we've seen people play around here."

"You know, even you agreed to play. Are you really giving up so easily? Just because Carleen found out?"

Katherine massaged the back of her neck with both hands and sighed loudly. "Just...don't breathe a word about this game to anyone, okay? Not even your best friend, not your lover, not even your sister."

"I won't." Her sister already knew about the game, but she wasn't going to tell Katherine that. Besides, like her sister said, New York was a big city, and she had promised to keep it quiet.

"Carleen doesn't tolerate this kind of behavior in her office. Every single one of us will be fired and without a reference to boot. It'd be hard to get a job in this town with that hanging over your head. Be careful."

Madeline shivered as she considered the possibilities of being untethered to her job in DC. "I will. Thanks for warning me."

"You can choose to quit if you like. It might not be worth it, especially for someone in your position," said Kat. She uncrossed her arms and relaxed the tension in her face.

"Are you trying to get me to quit? Trying to win the game by subterfuge?"

Kat drew back, as if she had tasted something awful. "Nice. ... oh never mind. Don't count yourself the winner yet, Madeline."

Chapter 11

After a long day at the office dealing with big egos, slow interns, and her own crazy schedule, Madeline was glad to be going to the PRSA meeting. She hopped on the Metro and, luckily, found a seat during the business rush hour. She wasn't exactly thrilled to be mingling without her friend Jeannie. She couldn't make it tonight, but she was excited to see Ewan afterwards.

The crowd would be mostly business since it was happy hour, so she didn't bother changing her clothes. And it wasn't like she was going on a date with Ewan. They were just meeting up so she could return his jacket. Even still, that morning, she had chosen an outfit that was mostly business and a bit flirty: a light brown and pink plaid mini skirt with a light pink buttoned silk shirt. She decided to wear her old-fashioned lace garters. It was too hot to wear a jacket, so she had left that at home.

On the Metro, Madeline pulled out her phone. She cruised by the Match app and double checked her date set up for Thursday, the fundraiser named Philip. *Check.* She closed the app and considered opening her work email, but instead, she opened up her e-book, and found herself lost again in the world of 18th century Scottish Highlanders.

This time, though, the image of Ewan in his kilt kept filling in the space of the male protagonist. She would never admit it to anyone, but she loved historical fiction with a dash of daring and romance.

Was there going to be romance tonight, she wondered? *Give it a rest Asher.* She wanted to denigrate the idea of romance: that it never happened, that it wasn't real, but after talking to her dad, she decided to quiet the voice---this one time---and let her gut decide if Ewan was trustworthy.

The Clarendon Grill was more of a low-key sports bar than a stylish city bar. A baseball game played on the television and there was a hearty selection of beer. She ordered the happy hour white wine from a roving waiter. She didn't like red after a long day at work. Besides, it stained her teeth if she had more than one glass. Madeline saw one of her acquaintances from the

PRSA and went up to say hi. She glanced around the bar to see if she knew anyone else, or if she could find Ewan.

Maybe she could find a random fundraiser to kiss for the BINGO game. The Netherlands Carillon was a fifteen-minute walk away. She'd win BINGO and be on her way to Vegas.

She brushed it aside. Deep inside, she knew if she played BINGO that her life would go down one path, and if she chose not to play BINGO---whatever that meant---her life would tumble down another. One path meant known quantities, a solitary life, but the other path, the path of trusting someone, could lead to heartbreak. Both were hard, but she didn't know which was worse.

Give it a rest Asher. Have a glass of wine. Enjoy the evening. Trust your gut.

She relaxed and started into a conversation with a fellow PR acquaintance about the difference between the advertising world and the political world. They were slight, but marketing and PR is about selling a product and not necessarily the truth, but a version of the truth, and giving a person the feels while doing it. Sometimes it felt like such a gimmick, a ruse, and other times there were honest moments when her job really mattered.

Like this upcoming gig in Vegas. She wanted to be

part of something big that helped reshape American industry. *Didn't she?* Images of flowers draped along rustic barn walls came to her mind. Men in tuxes and women in long, flowing gowns. Ewan in his kilt...She shook her head. She hadn't worked so hard to get where she was just to become a wedding planner at her dad's winery.

Out of the corner of her eye, she noticed Ewan. He was sitting at a bar stool and watching the Nationals play on TV. They scored a run, and she saw him cheer with a friend of his. He seemed solid, in the sense that he was tethered to the world in a way that she wasn't. She was more ethereal and fluid. He was someone she could hold on to, someone who wouldn't float away. *The way he held those babies in Guatemala.*

She liked the idea of being rooted. Ewan turned in his chair and looked over the crowd. He found her and waved. She waved back, then put up a single finger and mouthed, "one hour."

He gave her a thumbs up and winked before turning back to the game.

"Are you listening to me? You seem distracted," said Fiona, the woman she had been discussing marketing philosophy with.

"I'm sorry, I just saw someone that I'm supposed to meet up with later. But I agree with what you're saying. What do you think the future of marketing will be? Will it ever get back to being more factual? Perception seems to be everything right now." She laughed at her own little joke.

Fiona responded with a flurry of information and research she had read. Madeline nodded along as she made her case. The waiter finally brought her a glass of wine, and she wished she would have ordered two now since he was so busy.

More people chimed in on the conversation, and the topic expanded to include the idea of truth in marketing and what defined truth. Most of the time, these meetings were dry. The topics revolved around jobs—job openings, the latest cutting-edge ads, and so on and so on, never ending small talk—but this conversation stimulated her.

Someone tapped her shoulder, and she assumed it was going to be the waiter, so when she turned and was face to face with Ewan, she squeaked in surprise. Ewan double kissed her on the cheek, a decidedly European gesture. He smelled delicious—that orangey bergamot which weirdly reminded her of Ava. She could see him as a father. He did have a sort of sweetness about him, and, *damn, he looked good.* She wouldn't mind making babies with this man. She shook off the image of baby Mad-Ewans. *Give it a rest*

Asher. It's just a happy hour, don't marry the guy already.

"It's good to see you again." There was a directness in his gaze that made her quiver in anticipation.

Fiona was practically drooling over him. He had on his horn-rimmed glasses and his hair was loose, as if he'd been running his fingers through it.

"Hi. I'm Fiona," she said, forcing her way into the conversation. "I've known Madeline a while now. What's your name?" She took a step closer, trying to move in between her and Ewan.

Ewan leaned back just a smidgen. Madeline could tell he wanted to talk to her, but Fiona was barging her way in. Fiona was a looker, too. She was tall, model-thin, and blonde—the trifecta of beauty in DC. She wore a cotton shirt with a gorgeous diamond pendant that dangled at the top her ample cleavage. Fiona's hair was stick straight, and a little too bleached for Madeline's taste, but she wasn't judgmental about it.

Fiona was the kind of woman who made men's minds go blank, made their jaws hang wide open, and removed any capacity for intelligent conversation. She'd only seen a handful of guys who could handle her beauty with any aplomb, and most of them were gay. What she believed didn't really matter, what mattered was how Ewan responded.

"I'm Ewan. Nice to meet you, Fiona." He took a

small step back. It didn't come off as rude or offended but was clear in its meaning.

Madeline watched him carefully. His eyes never dropped to Fiona's cleavage, nor did they widen in desire. His smile was neutral.

"So, Ewan, what kind of work do you do?"

Oh, dear god that poor woman. She was about to drool, right here, in public. Madeline wanted to laugh, but she didn't. It was the first time she'd seen Fiona so overwhelmed by someone.

"You had a good meeting?" he asked Fiona.

"Yes." She reached out and tried to touch him lightly on the arm, but he moved out of the way, gliding away from her with the grace of a dancer.

"Fiona, it was so nice to catch up with you," Madeline said, cutting off the awkward silence.

"You as well. Any plans for after this?" she asked, directing her attention towards Ewan rather than Madeline. She flipped her hair back and bared her neck ensuring her cleavage was front and center.

"Madeline and I are going to watch the game together." Ewan brushed Madeline's forearm, and he focused on her, but the question was directed to Fiona. "Did you want to join us?"

Fiona looked to the TV monitor with abhorrence, then back to Ewan and Madeline.

"Thanks, but I just saw some friends from work. Maybe next time?" she said.

Fiona would be okay without them. She would certainly find more attention with her friends than with them. "We'll be over there."

"Smooth criminal," Ewan said under his breath. "I thought she was going to bonk me over the head and drag me home."

"I don't think Fiona likes to do the bonking, she prefers it the other way around."

"Clever girl. I never heard it that way before. Do you think that's the origin of the expression, bonking each other?" he teased, his eyes glittering with amusement.

"You think you're funny don't you?" Her hand was on her hip, but there was a smile on her face.

"I am funny," he said, with a mock expression of hurt. "Come on, let's head over to my spot. I'll introduce you to my friend."

As they walked through the crowd, he put his hand lightly on her waist, to help steer her through the crowd. The warmth of his fingers seeped through her clothes. Heat grew between them as if it were something palpable, something of substance. At the bar, Ewan's friend was chatting up some girl. They sat down and he turned towards her in all seriousness, like he wanted to ask her something important.

"Aren't you going to miss the game?" she asked.

"Meh. It's a game." He turned away to rub the handle of his beer. "Did you bring my jacket?"

"Your jacket! Oh no! I completely forgot."

"No worries. I'll get it next time. Your father's donation of wine helped us out a lot."

"I just saw him yesterday. You know he's here for six weeks. Helping to build an app for this charity. And he's taking a cooking class."

"Sounds like fun. Would you like to do that someday?"

"What? Build an app or take a cooking class?"

"A cooking class of course."

"With you or with my dad?" she asked.

"With me of course. We could invite him, too, I suppose."

"I'd like that. He really likes you, you know."

"He seems like a great guy."

"So how did you get involved with Orthopedics Every Family?"

He took a drink of his beer. Then, he took off his glasses and folded them, setting them on the bar. When he turned to look at her, she was drawn deeply into his blue eyes. The color was that of a stormy sky and there was a ring of sea green around his pupil, a yin-yang of light and dark. "It's a long story, but a lot of it has to do with finding yourself. Does that make any sense?"

"Like finding what you're made of?"

"That, but also finding a passion. It was a career I sort of stumbled upon, fundraising, but being in Guatemala made me the man I am."

"What do you mean?"

"Helping people, being part of a community, finding my purpose. I don't mean a spiritual purpose, there is that as well, but knowing where I fit, what I *really* wanted out of life."

Her whole life, no one ever'd talked to her this way. Men she had dated before were all about the dollar, the next big score, the expensive watches, the fancy car, the house. *Boring*. She knew what it was like to have everything: she had lived in her parent's mansion in San Francisco, attended celebrity parties at her dad's place in Napa, she rode to fancy parties in the Rolls with her best friend, and everyone had a Benz or BMW as the nanny car.

While she was grateful for the life her parents had given her, and she certainly wanted to maintain her lifestyle, she did not like the attitude that men had when trying to date her. Most of the time, they treated her like she was something to acquire. She wasn't arm candy like a fancy Rolex. She wasn't a Jaguar. She wasn't a piece of real estate. She was a person. She was a woman. Her dream was to marry someone who saw her, the real her.

"Then I met Bunny and Skip and started working with them. Now, here I am."

She shook herself out of her mild reverie. "And here you are. When are you headed back to Guatemala?"

"In a few days. I leave Friday morning actually. The Foundation likes to get us down there at least once a quarter, more if we have the funds."

She should have known better. Disappointment flooded through her. "How long will you be gone?"

"About a week this time, eight days to be exact. Dave's going to be there. How about you? I mean with the job. Do you love marketing? Working for the Congressman?"

Just a week. That wasn't so long. The Instagram photos showed longer trips in his past. She relaxed,."I do actually like my job. I don't know if it's my passion, my purpose, but I love being part of the political machine. It amazes me, really."

"How so?" he asked as if she were the only person in the whole room. Even when he took a sip from his beer, his gaze didn't waver from her. She found that she wanted to open up to him, to tell him everything. Well, everything except the whole BINGO thing. She would never tell him about that.

Madeline crossed her legs and pushed her hair back so it was out of her face. "Well, the fact that when I get home and watch the news, and they talk about Congress, I know it's right down the street from me, literally. I might be in a traffic jam because the president of the United States is coming home. I know people are annoyed by the traffic issues, but I think it's cool. Maybe it's because I grew up so far away from here. Nothing I ever experienced in my life was about politics. Now, I'm a part of it."

"Did you come out here looking for something in politics?"

"No. I started out with a law firm in DC and focused on in-house marketing. My friend Liz got a job with the Congressman first. When this job came up, she made sure my resume was seen. I still had to get through the interviews and all. That was grueling .... Now, here I am."

"Nice. Who you know makes or breaks it. So...tell me. How did your dad get involved with a winery? No offense, but your dad doesn't seem like the stereotypical winery owner."

"He was the CIO of Global Tech In San Francisco. He burned out and quit his job when I was sixteen, a junior in high school. That's when he bought the winery. He wanted to do something different. He likes growing things."

Ewan nodded along as she spoke. He looked over her shoulder, and his eyes widened for just a moment. His shoulders stiffened, and he turned away from her.

"What is it?"

"We need more drinks." He called the bartender over and placed a new order.

Madeline glanced behind her. A few from PRSA were still hanging about, but no one was looking their way.

He didn't turn back right away, but collected himself first by squaring his shoulders. "That's an ex-girlfriend over there. After I got back from Guatemala, and Guatemala is a whole other story, I started dating that girl over there. Everything seemed to be going well, but then she breaks up with me. She says I'm too into her. That she needs me to be more aloof. I didn't get her hints, so of course, she says to me *'we must not be soul mates'.*"

"What? That sounds like crazy talk. She said that?"

Ewan nodded. "I don't know if she was the one, but you know, I wanted us to be monogamous. I wanted to try to see if we could work. I guess I'm just old-fashioned."

"You want me to go kick her ass? I am a professional fencer." Madeline squared her shoulders into an offensive stance, ready to spar.

"No," he said, laughing. He scratched at the stubble under his chin. "I felt shitty for a long time after she broke up with me. I've had a lot of heartbreak." He smoothed down his shirt and began earnestly, "but what she did for me was clarify what I want. And what I want is that one person who understands me on a deep level. Someone I don't have to pretend with. Something real. No offense, I'm tired of the single life. I want to get married someday and have a family."

"Usually girls talk like that," Madeline said with a nervous smile. "You've been reading too many fairy tales I think."

"Don't you believe it can happen?" he asked her. He tilted his head to the side as his eyes narrowed, and his eyebrows crinkled into a single unit.

"Happily ever after? I'm not sure."

"Don't you believe real relationships can have a happily ever after?"

Madeline swallowed. She knew she had to answer that question for herself, but she didn't want to answer Ewan. She didn't want to accidentally set an expectation between them. Instead, she picked up his glasses and checked the lenses to see if they were clean. She untucked part of her shirt. "It's silk, it won't scratch the lens."

He nodded with an amused expression. The question hung in the air between them. She took a breath, ready to reply with something pragmatic and logical when a loud whoop erupted throughout the bar. Madeline whipped around for the source of the cheer, and Ewan pointed her towards the TV. The Nationals had scored a home run, and everyone was cheering. She finished cleaning his lenses and handed them back to him. "Better?"

"There's something I want you to see. Would you come with me?" Ewan asked, putting his glasses back on.

"Where are we going?"

"It's one of my favorite spots in all of DC. It's a surprise, okay. Come with me?"

"Alright."

He took her hand. She liked the way he held it, so matter of fact; like they were already together, like he had no uncertainty. The door of the bar shut behind them, blocking the sound of laughter and music. The street noise was quiet in comparison, almost calming. Ewan stopped. With his other hand, he raised it and caressed her cheek.

"You with me?" he asked.

Everything around her disappeared. All she could see was the blue of his eyes, the complexion of his skin. Her breath filled her lungs in a calming, sated rhythm.

It was the same as always, but there was something different. "I am."

HOLDING HANDS, they walked at a moderate pace. The humidity was wearing off in the evening, and cooler air brought them closer together. They didn't walk with purpose, but meandered arm-in-arm. He regaled her with stories of his adventurous youth exploring the moors of Scotland as a kid. She told him about the rigors of fencing and riding horses in Napa Valley.

They traversed through the Dark Star park, which was practically across the street from the Iwo Jima memorial and consequently the Netherlands Carillon, then through a short cement tunnel that had a decidedly sweet hobbit-like entrance.

Ewan didn't stop there. "Come on, we're almost there. How are your feet holding up?"

"My feet are fine. But where are we going? Are you going to tell me?"

Ewan stopped and stood close to her, touching noses almost. He brought his hand up and tipped her chin. "I want to tell you where we are going," he said in a husky voice. He moved both hands to the sides of her neck, just under the hairline. "But, it's a surprise."

Madeline closed her eyes and lifted her chin up so her throat was exposed. His fingers naturally followed the movement down to her collar bone and then they were gone. He was no longer touching her. Her eyes flew open, and he smiled at her.

She was so used to fast passion, kissing and hands everywhere, but this pace, this anticipation made her crazy. Madeline squeezed her thighs together to stem the throbbing need. She pouted at him, but he only smiled back. He didn't kiss her.

"If we start, we won't get to where I am taking you," he said.

"True."

Who was this guy? He definitely wasn't like anyone else she had ever met.

"Come on, we're almost there," he said, intertwining his fingers into hers and pulling her along. Ewan was leading her to the Iwo Jima park. Soldiers holding up the flag. Patriotic? Yes. Romantic? No. There was no way on God's green earth that he would be taking her *there*.

The Netherlands Carillon was right next to Iwo Jima memorial. The monument itself had a fantastic view of the city. But it wasn't a popular one, the only people who seemed to have heard of it stumbled upon it by mistake while visiting the Iwo Jima memorial or the even slimmer chance of having spotted it from the Arlington Cemetery.

She wondered why he would bring her to a place like this? The Netherlands Carillon was adjacent to it, but surely he didn't mean to take her there. And if he did bring her to the Netherlands Carillon, would she check in for her final BINGO?

Chapter 12

The Iwo Jima memorial is a stoic place. It's usually quiet, in deference to the soldiers who are shown saving the flag with the entirely likely possibility that the men died to protect freedom. Ewan's eyes were not on the Iwo Jima monument. He looked away from the statues and towards the Carillon.

No way. There was *no way* that Ewan would take her to the Netherlands Carillon. The chances of that happening were minute.

It also meant that she could claim a BINGO win if they kissed there. He was a fundraiser. The final and fifth kiss. A win. A chance to jump ahead in her career, to be a part of literally changing major industry from using fossil fuels to renewable energy.

Or she could be with Ewan. *Couldn't she?* If she wanted to be with Ewan, she could not check him in as a BINGO point. Not after their talk of destiny. He would never forgive it. Since she had met him, she wanted to think of him as someone she could love, but kept denying the possibility. Was he really something more? *No. Yes?*

Still undecided, she dug out the advice from her dad. *Trust your gut.* Nothing had triggered her defense mechanisms, and hers were easy to trigger. That was why short relationships were so easy to brush off, she didn't trust them to begin with. But, Ewan. He was a different character altogether. He was stoic. Sweet. A good man at heart. No matter what her sister said.

They stopped between the bronze lions which stood sentry. The air was spiced with the heady scent of lush greenery and jasmine. The Netherlands Carillon was a three-story tall open steel structure. At any point and time, she could have stopped, turned back to Iwo Jima and grabbed a nearby taxi. There was a decision to be made, but she didn't consciously choose, her body did.

Ewan brought her close to him and she put her arms around his waist. The heat of his body warmed hers even though the air was balmy. Ewan brought her hand between them and turned it palm up. He traced the lines in her hands again, but this time, he passed her palm and lightly traced his fingers against her bare skin up to her shoulder. She closed her eyes.

He kissed her. Softly at first. A nibble on her lip. His gentleness aggravated her and thrilled her in equal measure.

She opened her mouth to him. Tongues flared, teasing and then together, tasting and nipping at each other. He enclosed her in his arms. His hard cock brushed against her pelvis.

Earlier maneuvers to staunch her desire had done nothing; her pussy was wet, pulsing with desire. She imagined how he would spring from his pants, knowing what would happen after that. His hands danced from her waist and pressed against her ribs. Her nipples hardened into tiny buds that craved his attention. She arched forward, her body aching for release.

He slowed down his kiss and pulled away. She ground her teeth in frustration. She wasn't ready for him to stop.

"We're almost there. Come up with me."

Madeline only nodded. No words would come even if she tried. All she wanted was him, and now. His pace was aggravating, but she also relished the built-up tension, the yearning to pleasure her body.

They passed by the bronze lions, and Madeline swooped her hand along the hard metal mane. He led her up the three flights of stairs, looking back at her with hooded eyes that spoke of simmering heat and powerful release. Her legs nearly buckled as if she didn't even have the strength to hold herself. Walking up the stairs made her underwear rub against her clit, every motion driving her mad.

At the top of the metal stairs, he walked to the edge of a balcony. Above them hung fifty bells. In front of them was a gorgeous view of downtown DC with the Kennedy Center and the Washington Monument on the horizon.

"My favorite spot," he said, sweeping his hand toward the horizon.

She still could not believe it. He had brought her to this very spot, the very spot which---if she chose to Instagram it---would get her the BINGO prize. He stood next to her and draped his arm comfortably around her waist.

She dropped her purse at her feet. Her phone popped to the top. It would be easy to reach down and grab it for a selfie picture to Instagram. Before she could decide, he gently turned her body towards him and kissed her. His tongue slipped into her mouth, purposeful and strong. She gasped from the sudden pleasure. *Forget about the phone.* She met his tongue with impatient hunger. His hands were everywhere, on the back of her neck and running through her hair.

He stepped back slightly. A breeze came between them. He unbuttoned a single button from her pink blouse. Madeline breathed hard, her chest lifting and falling. Her nipples went from buds to hard pearls just from the anticipation. He unbuttoned the second button, then lightly pulled apart the shirt, exposing only her clavicle.

Ewan leaned down to give her a soft kiss. "This smells good. Rosemary?" The little hairs on her arm stood up.

"Grapefruit and rosemary."

"I like it." He unbuttoned the third and fourth button then pulled the fabric to the sides. He cupped her breasts, lifting them so the milky white skin curved like a hill. He did nothing to hide his desire, it was writ clear on his face. Ewan gazed up into her eyes, intent, knowing. "Beautiful. May I see them?"

She nodded. Being outside was daring and exciting. Someone might find them at the monument, and yet they were perfectly hidden away. He slipped his hands into the taut fabric of the bra and released her breasts. His eyes darkened. He took a nipple into his mouth and with his other hand pinched one. She moaned from the pressure and arched her back. He switched breasts, sucked harder and twisted her wet nipple. She moaned again, louder, and ran her hands through his wavy hair.

He grasped her nipple between his teeth and let it slide out slowly. It bounced back into shape. "We're going to get caught you know."

"I don't think so. And so what if we do?"

Ewan smiled, she could have sworn it was a take your panties off smile, and so she lifted the edge of her skirt.

"Face the railing." His eyes danced with naughtiness.

"Why, Ewan? Whatever are you going to do?" She fluttered her eyes at him and drawled her question out in her best Southern Belle imitation.

He kissed her again. It wasn't a kiss of frantic passion. He held her close to his body, his tongue explored her mouth, tasting her. She pulled back and caressed his cheek. Then she turned towards the railing, standing straight with her legs spread just enough. He pressed himself against her and reached around to fondle a breast. She leaned back against his strong chest, the summer breeze cool against her hot and naked breasts. He lifted her hair and kissed the back of her neck, while his other hand squeezed her breast, massaging, caressing, and pinching.

He rounded his strong hands around the curve of her hips, his fingertips lifting her skirt up. He stepped back, keeping a hand on her hip. Madeline leaned over slightly and held onto the railing.

He gasped.

"Beautiful."

He slid his fingers underneath the lace stays of her stockings, on the back of her thigh. He snapped them against her skin. Her pussy was throbbing, she was wet and the cool breeze only taunted her need. She tilted her pelvis back, towards him.

He slipped a finger under the edge of her lacy thong and traced it down the curve and into her crack. She stepped wider to give him better access. Her throbbing clit was exposed, but untouched. She looked at him over her shoulder trying to figure out what his plan was.

She was completely exposed to him, and anyone else who might wander along. He was studying her. The moment quivered in the air. Her clit swelled and grew harder. She pushed herself toward him, an obvious offering. The tension held in her body was exquisitely pleasant and painful.

With one finger, he touched her clit lightly, flicking back and forth. She wanted to scream *take me*. He flicked her clit harder. She arched her back and moaned, grinding against him and against the agony of his light touch. He stood up and kept one hand on her pussy, and his other hand reached around to pinch and twist a nipple. Her whole body rocked, pressing forward towards his hand holding a full breast and her hips pressed backwards to find more pressure for her clit.

"It's time to go." He pulled his hands away. Ewan pulled her skirt down and patted it.

She was shocked. Angry even.

He met her eyes and brought his hand up to his mouth and sucked his finger into his mouth. His eyes darkened with passion and more than a little mirth. "Delicious. Come with me," he said, straightening her bra back around her breasts and buttoning her blouse closed. She stood placidly, letting him dress her, letting him take care of her.

Her anger faded into desire. The actions made her feel safe with him, respected. No matter what her sister said about him, Ewan was not a player. She was just beginning to realize that she might be, though. At least she was always playing the odds, but did that make her a player? He tucked in his shirt while she ran fingers through her hair.

He pressed in close, pinning her between his hard, hot body and the railing. "We're not done yet."

"And what do you have in mind?"

"My apartment isn't far from here. I want to take you home and explore your body. Touch it. Taste it. I want you to be with me." He brought up her hand

and traced the lines of her palm then kissed her wrist.

Madeline only nodded in response. He could have asked in a myriad of ways. *I want you to come to my apartment* or *we're going to a hotel*, but he had said *I want you to be with me.* She knew that this wasn't just some fling for him. She picked up her purse and stuffed her phone securely inside. There was no way she would Instagram this kiss. And play BINGO? If he learned about the game, he'd be deeply hurt. And the last thing she wanted to do was hurt him.

THE WALK to Ewan's apartment should have taken only ten minutes, but it had taken them almost an hour from the bronze lion to the door. They had smacked each other's butts with flirtatious goofy grins, stopped for lingering kisses, intertwined their arms, and kissed each other with sweet tender pecks every other step.

She assumed that, once inside his apartment, the flurry of passion would start, that he would press her against the wall, and it would go from there, but he didn't. Once inside, he let go of her hand and headed into the kitchen. "Let me get you something to drink."

Madeline set her purse down and took off her shoes. So ... he was going to take his time. Her clit still throbbed from the passionate kiss at the Carillon. Her mind was drunk with love from the walk home. She lifted her skirt and slid a finger between her inner lips, rubbing her aching clit. While this did not fully satisfy her, it gave her a little relief from the constant pressure. Enough relief to enjoy a glass of wine with Ewan.

Her purse was unzipped, and she could see her phone peeking out. It had worked itself to the top, even though she had buried it under her wallet at the Carillon. She pulled it out and opened up Instagram. No one else had checked in with new kisses. She was still in the lead with four. But there was just no way she could do it. For him, for Ewan, she'd be willing to lose out on a huge career move. No more BINGO. No more stupid dating games. Would she give it up forever though? Was she willing to let go of her past and stand bravely in the face of love?

What's your gut say Madeline? Is he worth it?

She stuffed her phone back down and zipped it up tight as extra insurance. Old habits were hard to break. She focused on her surroundings instead. His apartment was a mish-mash of Guatemalan treasures like the framed art of Lake Atitlan and a hand painted gourd. On one wall, there was a framed picture of Babe Ruth pointing with his bat and another picture of a college soccer team. The place was clean, but not entirely picked up. A pair of athletic shoes and a soccer ball were heaped near the door. A stack of papers mixed with Outdoor magazines were piled on a dining room table. In spite of the slight messiness, things had an overall organization to them. There were no empty pizza boxes on his coffee table or crumpled beer cans littering his floor. The apartment was naturally cool and didn't stink of air conditioning. He called out for her to come into the kitchen.

"I don't have any wine left, but I have Prosecco."

"Italian champagne. Not bad, Ewan."

She took a sip of the fruity beverage and bubbles played along her mouth. Just what she needed, a perfect pick me up. She leaned across the granite countertop and looked him in the eye. "The champagne is nice. Thank you."

He leaned towards her and touched his nose to hers. "You're welcome."

He came around the countertop and took her hand. She stood to meet him. Her body brushed against his, her nose almost touching his lips. He lifted her chin to him and kissed her, a sweet kiss, as if he knew he had all the time in the world to give her what she wanted.

His hands went to each side of her face, his fingertips brushing away loose hairs. She wanted to feel his body and moved her hands up his arms, past his strong biceps, over his shoulders down his back, to his butt.

He pulled away and took her hand. Without a second glance, he led her to the bedroom.

She noticed small details as she walked by. Her purse on the sofa. The lines between the wide planks of the hard wood floor. A light was on in the bathroom. The tile walls were still moist from an earlier shower. The smell of his cologne mixed with the scent of tea tree oil and his natural musky scent.

In his bedroom, they stopped in front of the bed. He took off her shirt by lifting it over her head. She undid the clasp and let her bra fall. The skin of her breasts glowed in the soft light. He stood back and admired them.

He reached out and brought her in for a kiss. She unbuttoned his shirt as they kissed. Ewan moved to take it off over his head, impatient, but she pushed him back playfully. If he was going to make her go slow, then she was certainly going to make him wait.

She unbuttoned his shirt, shoving it over his shoulders and down his arms, letting it drop to the floor. Madeline brushed her hands over his curved chest, feeling a slight quiver of his muscles underneath her hand. She pinched his nipple. He swallowed hard in response.

Light blonde hairs covered his pectoral muscles and narrowed down to a thin line, disappearing into his pants. She kissed his nipple and rained a series of light kisses that followed his hairline down. Madeline unbuckled his belt and then unbuttoned his jeans. She pushed them down.

He stepped out of them. The tip of his cock was poking out of his checkered boxers. She ran her fingers between the elastic and his skin, peeling them off and shoving them to the floor. She dropped to her knees and took him in her mouth, licking at his salty skin, twirling her tongue around the tip.

Ewan leaned back, a sigh of desire escaping his mouth. He gently wound his fingers through her hair and guided her mouth off of him. He slipped his hands under her arms and lifted her up and away from him. "You first."

He unzipped her skirt, pushing it past her hips and to the ground. They collapsed on the bed together. His hard cock rubbed against her stomach. She knew she was in for a treat with his size—big enough to send waves of pleasure through her.

Madeline was on her back. Ewan lowered his body until he was eye level with her breast. He took a nipple into his mouth and pinched the other. She tilted her head back and moaned. He continued down until his lips grazed her belly. He pressed a finger into her belly button. She wasn't expecting the surprisingly sexy feeling that ran up her spine.

In a trail of wet kisses, he continued his exploration of her body. He reached her mound and stopped. He got up on his elbows and smiled at her.

Madeline gave him a sultry smile and slowly let her knees fall to the side. She opened herself up to him, offering him what he so obviously wanted. His hands slid down her thighs, so they rested on each side of her pussy. With his thumbs, he pulled the lips apart deftly and just looked at her. She watched his expression change to desire and wonder. He was seeing a part of her that no one else had ever taken the time to explore.

His head disappeared and his nose gently nudged her clit. She heard him take a deep breath. He was taking all of her in, the essence of her. Sweet tension built. She tried to close her knees, to contain the pressure, but he pushed them apart. His tongue swirled around her clit, lightly at first, until she was sure she'd go mad wanting him. He increased the intensity, then sucked her clit into his mouth. She cried out and grabbed the comforter with both hands. She tried to close her legs around him once more, but he pushed them out again, forcing her to be open to his view, to his mouth.

"Oh my god! Jesus Ewan, I can't take it, it's too, oh my God," cried out Madeline.

He continued sucking her clit, his tongue swirling around it. The pressure was exquisite. He slipped two fingers inside her. She cried out with pleasure, her breath fast and ragged. She tried, again, to squeeze her legs together. He firmly pressed them out with his elbows and sucked harder, his fingers pulsing in her vagina harder and faster, scraping upward toward her g-spot. He lapped up her juices as if he were starved.

Just as she was about to explode, he stopped what he was doing and shifted to his knees.

"What? Why?" she sputtered in short gasping breaths.

He hovered over her, grinning. His penis was hard as a rock and pointed north, leaning slightly towards her, as if it knew where to go.

He rolled a condom over his cock. She wanted to taste him again, to lick the salty ridges and pump him hard with her hands, but the condom was already on. She bit the corner of her lip, excited and ready for what was to come. A fresh flow of wetness covered her pussy, the folds sensitive to the barest of touch.

With a naughty smile, he pushed his dick down, towards her. She needed him inside her. She needed him to fill her. Now. She'd been so, so close. It wouldn't take long for him to send her soaring over the edge.

He teased her clit with the tip of his cock. She was so wet, hot juices dripped between her crack. She thrust her hips toward him, trying to position herself closer to him. He positioned himself over her, one hand on either side, and pushed into her, filling her. Her pussy wrapped around him.

He pulled himself completely out of her. She didn't want to let him go, but she knew what was to come would be worth her impatience. She looked down her body and watched as his dick slid back into her pussy, gasping at the sweet sensation of being stretched open. He came into her deep, to the root, and stayed there, savoring a moment before pulling back again, and thrusting into her again. With each movement, he dragged the length of his cock along her clit.

They started rocking back and forth, into and away from each other. Her swelling clit being fucked by his rhythmic pounding against her, the momentum propelling them towards release. He was deep inside of her, his throbbing cock touching her core.

She went from gentle moans to crying out to not caring who might hear her screams. "Take me! Ewan. Take me!" She dug her fingers into his back and squeezed her pussy tight against him, relentless, wanting to take him even deeper inside her. The pace quickened, he penetrated harder and faster with each stroke.

She rocked her hips to match his pace. His speed changed to those final, wild passionate thrusts, as he was about to come and no longer had control of his own body. He gripped her body in a tight hug. His penis quivered inside her with an animalistic pulse. A wave of sheer electricity zinged through her body, and she cried out with the pleasure, his body absorbing the shock of her orgasm, wave after wave.

They stayed locked together. Two different parts of a wheel, they fit perfectly together.

"That was ... that was ... I don't even have words for it." He appeared shocked by his words, bee-stung, or rather, love stung. "I think I ..." He didn't finish the sentence, but looked at her, his eyes intense.

"What the hell did you do to me? I have never had an orgasm like that before."

Ewan pulled out, but kept her close, keeping her protected in his arms. He kissed her on the lips, then on the forehead. They stayed like that, quiet and together until Madeline thought she might fall asleep.

He stirred next to her, gently pulling stray hairs off her face. "I'm going to get something to drink for us. Don't you dare move a muscle, I'll be right back?"

"Can I come with you? I'm starving."

"Anything you like."

They stumbled into the kitchen, both buck-naked and comfortable in each other's presence.

"Twice in one night?" she asked him while buttering up a piece of cinnamon raisin bread.

"Maybe. But damn, girl, you took everything out of me. It might take a week to replenish."

"It better not."

"Don't you worry, baby." He pulled her close to him and held her tight. He kissed her eyes closed and then her forehead. "It definitely won't take a week."

She dropped her toast on the ground and kissed him back.

Chapter 13

The next morning, she awoke refreshed. Ewan's body curled around hers, and her legs intertwined into his. She hadn't slept that well in years and never that well with another person.

He woke up and squeezed his arms tight around her. "Don't leave yet."

Madeline closed her eyes. She inhaled his musky morning smell, a faint tinge of orange bergamot still lingered. Even his morning breath felt like home. Everything about him. Her upper arms tingled, she didn't want to leave, she didn't want to ever leave. She was protected in his strong arms and safe from the whole world.

His hands cupped her breast. "Beautiful."

She moved her hands down his back and cupped his ass. "Beautiful."

His hips curled into hers. His hard dick pressed against her thigh. The tip already moistened with pre-come.

"You have a beautiful penis Ewan." It was a simple statement of fact.

"Ha. It's multipurpose too." He moved her shoulders so they were flat on the bed. She opened her legs for him. He slipped a finger inside her.

"You're wet for me." He lifted his finger and licked her juices. A look of bliss came over his face which excited her. He rolled onto her and lifted his hips. His beautiful dick knew exactly where to go and the tip was ready at her opening.

But this time, he didn't go slowly. He rammed into her, hard. She yelped in response. Her breasts bounced and her nipples hardened.

She arched her back, matching his thrusts with her own hunger and need. She pulled her legs up over his shoulders so he could go deeper and smirked at his look of surprise. And deeper he went, thrusting, ramming the whole of him into her.

She grunted against him, squeezing herself, wanting to take him inside of her, wanting her own orgasm. The last thrust was fierce. She bit her lip and the waves of ecstasy washed over her body like ocean waves coming down on her, smattering her thoughts, smashing her care, and she cried out, her sound raspy and edged with passion.

"You are incredible," he said, breathing as hard as if he'd run an 8-minute mile. "We fit together you know, our bodies belong together. We're meant to be." He traced a line around her peach colored areola, over her shoulder and down to her waist.

She closed her eyes and let herself bask in his appreciation of her body. She wanted to let his sincerity wash over her, to stay away from the cynicism that usually popped up after sex.

"Can you call in sick? I'd love to spend the day with you before I go to Guatemala."

"I wish I could," she said, "but I have two dead-lines the end of this week." She actually had three---the BINGO deadline---but she decided then and there that she was not going to win. For the first time in her life, she would lose. Maybe this time, it was better to let someone else win. Cheyenne or whoever went would do great in Vegas. She kissed him, then stood up and pulled the sheet with her, leaving him naked.

"Ewan, love, I do have to work. I'm late as it is. I'll be in the shower."

She saw his penis stir, hardening, and instinctively aimed straight for her.

"Alone. I'm really late," she said, looking pointedly at him.

"When do you get off work? I want to see you again as soon as possible."

"You'll have to call me to find out," she said with a naughty grin.

"Don't make any plans. I'm taking you out to dinner tonight."

AFTER HER SHOWER, she took a cab home. In her bathroom, she did her hair and changed into a gray pencil skirt and a crisp white cotton shirt. Before she put her shirt on, she smelled the crook of her arm. His smell still lingered on her body, and she smiled dreamily at the events of the evening and that morning.

She texted her friend Jeannie to cancel their happy hour to celebrate her new job and said she would make it up to her. Her phone rang. She looked at the panel, thinking it might be Ewan already, but the letters read AUNDREA.

Oh shit. Madeline almost didn't pick up, but she knew that if she didn't, Aundrea would be relentless. She always picked up the phone, especially in the morning on a work day.

"Hi Aundrea. How are you?" she asked, trying to sound nonchalant.

"Emily is finally back. Her foot is better, and she took Ava to the park. It's so nice to have a break."

"Didn't you have a backup?"

"Can you believe the agency was overbooked? They had no one. And, Ava had a hard time sleeping the past few nights. I'm running on four cups of coffee here."

"You'll be okay."

"I will. I love her so much, but I was very happy to see Emily this morning. But now, I can't sleep. How's Dad? Did you see him this week?"

"Yeah, his cooking class is awesome. He made me a killer Pad Thai." She was about to tell her that he had suggested divorcing Mom, but hesitated. If her sister got involved, she would manhandle the whole event, either calling up Mom to yell at her or argue with Dad. It'd get messy.

Messy. Another reason not to tell her about Ewan. She didn't want her sister involved. Aundrea would tell her what to do. That was what she always did. Then, she would proceed to tell her what a schmuck he was. Madeline didn't want to hear it, not after last night.

Instead of always being the little sister and always doing what big sister told her, she wanted to choose for herself. She wanted Ewan. She smiled at the memory of his wild hair and knowing what was to come that evening.

"Anyone there? Hello? Do you think they'll get a divorce? They are hardly ever together."

"What are you talking about? Mom and Dad?" Madeline asked. Her sister was uncanny sometimes, saying exactly what Madeline was thinking. They might as well have been born twins for how intuitive they were with each other.

"It doesn't sound like you are at work yet. It's really late for you. Why are you running late?"

Madeline rolled her eyes. She didn't stand a chance with her sister. Trying to establish her independence with Aundrea, who had taken charge of her since she was born, was going to be anything but easy. But she had to try. "I slept in late."

Weak Asher. But something.

"You are a light sleeper. You've been a light sleeper since the third grade. You never sleep in unless you were drunk the night before, and your voice doesn't have that hangover edge."

"What is this? The Spanish Inquisition? It's only nine thirty."

"Were you with Ewan last night?"

How could she possibly have known? *Damn it.* "Aundrea, come on."

"You were! Madeline, what the hell are you doing? He is a giant dick. I told you to stay away from him."

"Knock it off Aundrea! I am trying to get to work. I'm late and I don't need to be frazzled."

"Fine. Whatever, Madeline. But, we are talking about this later."

"There's nothing to tell. I'm *with* Ewan."

"He has a girlfriend in New York, well" she paused, looking for the right word, "had. He had a girl-friend. Her name is Deirdre."

Ewan would never date a girl named Deirdre. No way.

"Dave *knew* him in Guatemala. Said he was always with a girl. Dave bragged about him, said he was like a stallion, you *know* what that means."

"Thanks Aundrea. Thank you for completely screwing up my morning. I have to go."

"Deirdre told me that she had a pregnancy scare. When she told Ewan, apparently, he threw a couple of hundreds in her face and told her to take care of it. He's a class A douche bag Madeline."

Madeline had slung her briefcase over her shoulder and had just lifted her hair out from under the strap. She was about to leave her apartment and stopped. "There is no way that happened. That isn't even close to what Ewan is like. Or even what he would say."

"Are you sure? You positive he didn't play you, that he wasn't looking to screw you? Dave said he was *super* busy in Guatemala. It all adds up. He's one of *those* guys. Madeline, you can't see him again."

"Stop telling me what to do! You're sick you know that. Besides, who is this Deirdre? Did you just make her up so you could stay in control of me?"

"I didn't tell you because I didn't think you'd ever see him again. And Deirdre is a friend. We go out for happy hours."

"So you're willing to ruin my life because of someone you go out to happy hours with? You don't really know her, do you?"

"Ruin your life? Please. You always blow everything way out of proportion. Besides, why would she lie? This happened way before you and Ewan, it's not like she said it out of jealousy. It's the truth. Did you know he is leaving again for Guatemala with Dave? He probably said that to Deirdre so he could be free to do, you know, whatever he wants. *To be a stallion.*"

Madeline's mouth dropped with a sharp intake of breath, like someone had just sucker punched her with an upper hook. She knew he was leaving for Guatemala, he had told her in the bar last night that he was leaving Friday.

Was Aundrea right about Ewan? Past behavior of men that she had dated would indicate that Aundrea was closer to the truth than she was. *Was her gut that wrong?* But she would not give her sister the pleasure of having the upper hand and collected herself. "Yes. I. I knew that."

"Right. Why didn't you listen to me? I told you to stay away from him."

"You're not my mom Aundrea. I don't need you to tell me what to do. I can take care of myself."

"Like the way I looked after you when Damon cheated on you? This big sister *is* looking out for you. Is this how you're going to look after Dad?"

"What is that supposed to mean?"

"I know how to take care of people. I am good at it. And you don't. You just keep messing up. You can't even properly take care of Dad."

Madeline threw the phone onto the bed, wishing she had an old-school wall phone she could slam down hard. *Screw her sister.* Who the hell did she think she was, talking to her like that?

And Ewan? How dare he do this to her? Aundrea wouldn't make up something just to hurt her. Not something like that. And this Deirdre person--why would she have lied to Aundrea about something like that? There was no reason for it. What kind of man throws money at a woman who's pregnant with his child? The man she knew held babies in Guatemala. He talked about things that mattered, like finding purpose. He wasn't a windbag of words. *Or was he?*

Had Ewan played her utterly and completely? He had been so suave, so easy going...clearly had plenty of practice. She picked her way through the precious night and morning. He had been very attentive to her needs, to every twitch of her body, ensuring she had every bit as much of pleasure as he took from her.

Every caress, every kiss, every moment, now casting each second into suspicion, and questioning his motive. He hadn't said anything about love. Or the future. Or what next. He'd just asked her to stay the day, so they could fuck all day before he went back down to Guatemala. Was that all he wanted? To hit one last buffet before going into the wild?

Damn it. She'd been so stupid to fall for it.

Not again. She was not going to be stupid about a man again. The only way to play the game of love, was to play it smart. She wasn't going to hope that she'd turn around and find out he was a good guy after all. Men don't change their spots.

What a dumb and stupid saying. But accurate. She'd been duped. Fooled. Taken for a ride.

She picked up her phone and opened up Instagram. She would check in at the Netherlands Carillon. She would win BINGO. She would go to Vegas. She would forget about Ewan.

But...she couldn't press the button.

She clenched her fist and let out a frustrated grunt. She closed Instagram and opened up the Match.com app.

Fuck Ewan. Screw him.

She emailed her date, requesting that they meet somewhere in Arlington. She'd have her fifth BINGO kiss by tomorrow night. She would go to Vegas, and she would forget about Ewan. *Ugh.* Tonight, that stupid foul mouthed sweet talker pig-headed jerk wad was going to experience real pain on their dinner date. But she couldn't yell at him now, she didn't have time, she had to get to work.

Chapter 14

How she got to the conference room was beyond her. Her mind had been transported somewhere else, and replaced by this other, angry and outraged woman who had the ability to extend her claws like some kind of wolverine. She yelled at the cab driver, glared at the security guy coming into the building, and cut in front of someone at the water fountain.

Madeline slammed open the door to the conference room, plopped down in her chair, and scowled at the walls. She was glad to be alone but knew that Chloe and Kat would be coming shortly to the meeting. The best thing to do was just not think about Ewan or her sister right now. She had a job to do. Madeline adjusted her computer on the table and straightened out her notebook. She took a deep breath and adjusted her countenance to be more neutral.

She got a text from Ewan.

Ewan: Thinking of you still. I'm coming over tonight to pick you up. What's your address?

Her stomach clenched. Does he know Deirdre's address? *The way he touched her.* She might throw up.

Madeline took a sip of water to calm her nerves. She had a plan in mind, but if she was going to be able to tell him off tonight, she had to get through the day. Katherine came into the conference room first, then Chloe.

Carleen followed the ladies into the room. She was a petite woman, in her early fifties with light gray hair that almost looked silver. *What did she want?* Carleen was Katherine's boss and Link's aide de camp. Madeline admired her Manolo Blahnik silk satin crystal embellished pumps with a stiletto heel. Carleen was all business, but her sweet style in shoes let you know she'd dance all over your ass if you messed up. Madeline straightened out her paperwork on the table.

"Hello ladies. Go ahead and sit, I'm not going to stay. I just have a few things to clear up."

Katherine and Chloe didn't waste any time and found a place at the conference table.

"First, Katherine, thank you for letting me cut into some of your meeting. I know time is of the essence, so

I'll get right to it. There are a lot of moving parts to this office. Katherine and the hearing, which thankfully is almost over," she said pointedly looking at Kat. "Chloe, you're doing a great job with everything too. Madeline, your work is impeccable, as always."

"Thanks Carleen. I met Liz last week," said Madeline. Having a specific task to accomplish that took her mind from Ewan calmed her down. "I finished up the press release for the Chinese Ambassador's visit. We made sure to mention the industrial angle and our new possible trade agreements that will help boost the economy and jobs. We found a great human-interest angle. Both their mothers were teachers, so they are going to collaborate together to find sister cities and possibly an exchange program."

"Good to hear. There will be another update about Liz, but not just yet. When the time is right. That's it ladies. I just wanted to make sure you know that I'm very happy so far with the way everything is running as it should. Smooth and on the *up and up*." She made sure to look in the eye of every woman at the table.

"We're handling it," said Kat.

"Good. That's what I want to hear. I've got to run." Carleen opened the door and walked off, without closing it behind her. Chloe stood up and closed the door.

"And how is it going with SUNFLOWER? Do we

have a winner for Vegas yet? The deadline is in two days," said Katherine. "I can't wait for this game to be over. It's going to give me a heart attack."

"No. There's no one yet. Cheyenne and I both have four marks. I'm sure one of us will win it in the next 48 hours."

Chloe smiled and looked blissful. Madeline knew vaguely that Chloe and Harrison, the environmental lawyer working for them on the SUNFLOWER project, were fast becoming a hot item. She glared at her. Madeline's phone chimed. Her Match date just sent her confirmed that Arlington was fine. Where would they meet?

The only way she'd get her last BINGO spot and win is if she kissed him at the Netherlands Carillon. Her stomach gurgled, and she almost threw up. She pushed it down and ignored it. She'd get her kiss Thursday. Win BINGO. Go to Vegas. *Forget about Ewan.*

This time, it wasn't about winning and beating out the competition. This time it was about forgetting how much a heart can hurt. She should have listened to her sister in the first place. Now she was in this mess with Ewan and she had to clean it up, not her sister, not Dave, her. Madeline texted him her address. Nothing less nothing more.

She got an immediate response.

Ewan: I can't stop thinking about you. The way you taste so good.

She picked his text apart. Why focus on how she tastes? She had been so wrong about him. He's thinking about her, but not who she is. Madeline rubbed her forehead. She wished she had checked in at the Netherlands Carillon after all. At least she wouldn't be in this painful position. Maybe she'd end up a jaded old cat lady, but that was better than ever having her heart broken again. She had only seen him twice in her entire life, and, yet, her whole life had changed. She swallowed hard. Ignorance was bliss after all and she closed her eyes wishing she could have had at least one more day of happiness with Ewan.

"This game is so strange, people seem to be falling in love instead of actually playing BINGO," Chloe said off-hand.

Madeline raised her eyebrows and started to chew on her pen. *Love.* She chewed harder on her pen leaving bite marks.

"We have all the legislation drafts ready to go. It's just a matter of deciding who is going to be there," said Katherine. "We'll need to start our PR work on that angle as well, making sure that the constituency sees the benefits alternative energy production will have for our state."

"That will be easy. There are so many opportunities for not only manufacturing, but also in IT, implementation, sales ... I mean we could prep this in a number of ways. The best is a narrative that resonates with the populace—creating jobs, making money, and doing the right thing. The possibilities are endless."

Katherine tapped the table with her fingertips. "The Congressman will want PR for small businesses as well, how investing in alternatives will save them money, which in turn will allow them to expand their own business."

"Also, we need to make sure we reiterate the safety of alternative energy along with its reliability for target markets," said Madeline.

"Sounds like a great plan. Let us know when you can get started," said Katherine.

"Will do. Print, radio, web, what are our platforms?" asked Chloe.

"Any platform we can utilize, we will," said Madeline, a little irritated at the question. She tried being patient—Chloe was a law school intern, after all. "I'll review the target audiences and send out the master plan."

"That's a wrap then," said Katherine. "Chloe. Stay here. We have extra work to talk about. I spoke with Pierce and have some changes for the bill."

Madeline closed her computer and started to put away her notebook. She picked up her pen, now with deep teeth marks on it. She took a deep breath and tossed it into her bag.

"Are you okay Madeline? You seem a little ... stressed," said Chloe.

"I'm fine," Madeline said, not making eye contact. She stood up and put her bag over her shoulder. It swung around and hit the chair. It almost knocked her over. She grabbed the handle of the bag to stop it from swinging.

"Yes. I'm fine," she said again, but this time making eye contact with Chloe. From the corner of her eye, she could see Katherine's lips had disappeared into a tight line. She had her hand on her hip.

"You sure? I need my team running smoothly," said Katherine.

"Don't worry about me. I have it under control." She readjusted her bag once again and stalked out of the room.

Wednesday seemed to never end. She didn't want to see Ewan; she didn't want to break up with him, didn't want to acknowledge that he wasn't the one. It was an emotional rollercoaster, and she wanted off. She didn't even want to yell at him and was rethinking her plan from the morning. Once Madeline got home, she locked herself in the bathroom even though no one else was there. The unnecessary action made her feel even more private.

She examined her haggard-looking face in the mirror. Her eyes looked like they were about to bug out of her head. Her hair was disheveled. Nothing about her was right. Her breath caught in her throat. She smoothed her hands over her throat, trying to swallow whatever it was that had lodged itself. When that didn't work, she coughed. All she wanted was to breathe easy again.

But she could smell him everywhere on her skin, in her hair. She wished she could be blissfully in his arms again—sated and happy. Her inner thighs were still sore from their amazing love making last night and this morning.

Madeline wanted to collapse. Her knees were weak and on the verge of buckling. How was she going to make it through the evening? How was she going to tell the one person who made her believe love could be real that he was a complete piece of shit?

Didn't he deserve the benefit of the doubt? Her dad's advice came back to her. *Trust your gut.*

Her gut was nothing but a knot. There was a tiny speck of her that still believed Ewan was a good guy. But, she trusted Aundrea, too. And really, Aundrea had always been there for her. She'd been the one to hold her tight and get her through heart-aches. How could she trust her gut when it came to less than five days of knowing someone?

Madeline could barely hear the quiet voice over the angry ruminations in her head. She had been hurt so many times that it was natural for her to go straight into an offensive position. Maybe instead of launching a missile of anger at him, she should calm down and find out what his story is. Her sister might not know everything. Her sister might have exaggerated the account. Maybe Deirdre was a lunatic and made the whole thing up. Her body wanted Ewan, her heart begged her to listen, but her mind was a solid wall of protection.

When the doorbell rang, she buzzed him in even though her heart pounded, sweat beaded up in her underarms, her mouth was dry. She wanted to bolt; she wanted to run away and never look back. But she couldn't. He was on his way up the elevator now, and she was about to see him again through the filter of Aundrea's news.

He knocked on the door. She didn't want to answer, but she did want answers so she tried to relax herself and at least appear like a normal person. She stared at the closed door willing him to go away. Wishing that she was anywhere but right there at that moment. After waiting as long as she dared, she opened the door to him.

There he was. His smell came in first. She wanted to melt but straightened her back with resolve.

He grinned at her as he came inside. "*You* look great."

He kissed her lightly, she kissed him back, her body in shock. Madeline didn't know whether to laugh or cry. Unable to say anything just yet, she led him to the kitchen where she could keep herself busy pouring him a glass of wine. Before she could get out the glasses, he held out a gift to her. Surprised, she fingered her collarbone with one hand and held onto the counter for support, hoping she didn't look ridiculous. She wasn't expecting this.

Madeline opened the box and found a round jewelry case made of jade.

"It's hand-carved," he said.

She rubbed her finger across the polished green stone. She wanted to remember him as she did this morning, his hands caressing the curve of her waist, his lips softly kissing her arm. She clenched her jaw and swallowed. Whatever was stuck in her throat was still there.

He didn't notice her aloofness. "I leave for Guatemala on Friday. But it's only for eight days. I'm going to miss you." He took a seat on a bar stool. "And by the way, I'm meeting Dave at the airport in Dallas, where we both have a layover."

"I know." She swallowed again, but the lump stayed lodged.

"I know this is kind of jumping ahead a bit," he said, looking intently at her. "But, I think it'd kill me if you were with anyone else. I want us to be monogamous. Right now. Just you and me."

Madeline's head spun and focusing on anything was impossible. The whole situation was totally surreal. For the first time in a long time she had actually experienced something for a man beyond the 'I'm here for a good time' vibe. But she knew her sister's truth about him. Dave's stories. All of it pointed to a man who would not wait for her.

"I heard all about Guatemala Ewan," said Madeline, sharper than she had intended to. "I heard all about your time as a big old stud on the farm."

He stepped back. He blinked and his eyes narrowed in on her, sharp and focused. "What are you talking about?"

"Dave told Aundrea how you were screwing just about every girl you could get your hands on."

"Dave said that?"

"And my sister says you have a girlfriend in New York. Deirdre. Was she pregnant?" Madeline glared at him. It took everything she had to throw down and be a bitch when she wanted to feel safe in his arms.

Ewan closed his eyes and rubbed them with his fingertips. He shook his head and let out a long, weary sigh. "Madeline, your sister has the story wrong."

A little prickle of defensiveness on behalf of Aundrea made her hackles rise. "She wouldn't lie to me."

Ewan held up his hands placating. "I didn't say she *lied*. I don't know where she got her story from. But, will you hear me out?"

Madeline didn't move. Their eyes locked together. She evaluated him, his body language, internally gauging whether his story was worth her time. Ewan had protected her from that creep at the Hamptons party. His gentle tracing of her hand on the beach and his not looking to screw her from the first second he laid eyes on her were proof he wasn't *that guy*. Their long conversation at the Clarendon Grill, and the way he treated her and her body the previous night and this morning were not just an act. He was genuine, the real deal.

"Yes, but I need a glass of wine." It was as though she was out of her body, watching from above. The woman in charge was going to make damn sure that he wasn't a charlatan, like the other guys who had broken her heart before, abused her trust.

She poured herself a glass and one for Ewan too. He left it on the table, his eyes still steady on hers. Madeline sat on a barstool and coolly returned his gaze.

"I'll not be drinking when I tell you this. I want you to know that what I am about to say, I say it because it's the truth."

Her eyes watered and she blinked to clear the tears away. Most of the time, when she confronted a man, they would storm out, run off, or try to quell her fears with a forceful but ineffective embrace. This was different. She had no defenses against this. Her heart begged her to keep an open mind, but her mind was very close to shutting him and his words out.

"In Guatemala, I did see a lot of women. It's a long story why though, and I'm not sure if I'm ready to tell you. I can see you're angry and upset, and I'm not sure you'll actually hear anything I have to say right now." His breathing remained steady but his voice wavered, as if he might cry. "I am not going to see or sleep with anyone else when I am in Guatemala." He swallowed hard, and she could see him silently pleading with her.

A twinge of guilt came over her. It's not like she wasn't dating around too. She already had a date set up for tomorrow night. If he knew she was playing BINGO, the whole conversation would be different.

"What about Deirdre?" she asked quietly. While

she understood that the actions in her own life might be hypocritical, she also was not dating anyone seriously.

He looked genuinely shocked and confused. "Deirdre and I broke up almost six months ago. I didn't feel it was fair to her to continue the relationship. It was more complicated than that, she was ..."

"Was she pregnant?"

His mouth opened, and his eyebrows lifted into high arches. With a deep breath, he visibly composed himself. "She told me she was. I wanted to help, but then she disappeared."

He wasn't denying they were in a relationship. He wasn't trying to hide anything. The heavy lump returned to her throat, swelling. She scratched her temple and swallowed hard trying to clear it out.

"I tried to call her, to make sure she was okay, but I never heard from her again." Ewan stepped closer to her. He cupped her face gently and kissed her on the lips. "Even if she'd really been pregnant, it doesn't mean I'd be *with* Deirdre. I never loved her. I love you. I know it hasn't been long. I admit I've been around. But with you, I *just know*. From the moment I met you, Madeline."

Warm electricity spread from her arms, over her shoulders, into her back and up her neck.

"Do you trust me?" he asked.

"I don't know," she said honestly. She found that she didn't respond to him in anger, to protect herself from him, or say yes out of lust to simply give in to her desire.

"Ask Dave anything you want. Call him every day for an update."

Madeline smiled at him, knowing Dave would tell her the truth, even if it annoyed the crap out of him, having to talk to her every day.

"When I get back, let's try being together. You need time to catch up to me." He held her hand again, massaging her palm, "I just found you. I can't let you go just because you heard a lie about me."

"I don't know if I can, Ewan."

"Wait for me. Please. I won't be gone long."

Madeline didn't know what to say. Everything in her body wanted to say yes, to tell him that she trusted him, that she loved him too, that he was right, they fit perfectly. But no words came out.

"I need time Ewan. I need time to think about all this."

"Okay, okay," he said. "Call Dave every day. He'll tell you."

"I will. Ewan, I'm sorry, I can't have dinner with you tonight."

"I know, love. I'll give you space."

She looked through her tear-filled eyes, willing

herself not to cry, that she couldn't cry. But if she spoke, the tears would come.

"You're not the only one who's had their heart broken, and there's not enough time for me to tell you my story the way I need to. When I get back? I'll be around for a while, so we can really get to know each other." He pulled her in for a hug. His warmth seeped through her clothes. She wanted nothing more than to stay with him.

He kissed her tenderly on the lips, then released her from their embrace. He cupped her face in his palms, forcing her to look at him. "I'm coming back for you."

She could get lost in that ocean of blue.

I'm coming back for you. His words danced around in her head.

Madeline couldn't move. She blinked her eyes. With another blink of her eyes, he had turned. And with a third blink, he was gone. Somewhere in all that, she heard the door shut.

Chapter 15

Thursday morning came fast. Madeline didn't sleep well after Ewan left. When she did, it was restless and she kept dreaming that he was next to her. The bed was warm and safe, and she didn't want to get out. She did not want to go to work. She didn't want to face anyone. But she forced herself to get up and do what she always did.

Physically, she made it to work. She was there but not present. The day passed excruciatingly slowly. Every conversation she had slipped from her consciousness. Words swept around and through her without making any real sense to her. Her mind was still in her apartment reliving the last conversation she had with Ewan. His words resonated between every single conversation she had that day.

I'm coming back for you.

Even though she had showered, the smell of orange bergamot still lingered on her skin. And when she smelled him, she remembered the intensity of her pleasure. Their pleasure. The contrast of her exquisite happiness clashed against the damning words of her sister. They say words will never hurt you, but Madeline's entire body ached as if she had been pummeled. She didn't want to talk to her sister and had ignored her last two calls.

Getting Ewan off the brain was more difficult than she had anticipated. Nothing worked, not even a text from Philip, the guy she met on Match and had a date with that evening. He was a fundraiser too, and that was all that mattered. She didn't even care what company he worked for. He was cute, at least his picture was cute, but another voice in her mind staunchly said that he wasn't Ewan, that she should cancel the date. She should wait eight days for Ewan to get back from Guatemala.

What could happen in eight days? She tried to approach it logically. The most likely scenario is that she would hear from Dave about what a loser he was. *Then where would she be?* She will have wasted all that time hoping that he would turn out to be a good man on top of losing BINGO, which would cause the loss of an important job opportunity. She was going on the date with Philip, even if she had to force herself. Kissing him at the Netherlands Carillon was an attempt to erase her kiss with Ewan.

At home, she went into her bedroom and looked for something to wear for the date. In her laundry basket was the outfit she wore with Ewan. A smell of musky sex lingered. She picked up the clothes and threw them into the laundry machine. She slammed the door closed and turned the machine on. The only way out of this situation with Ewan, the only way out that would hurt her the least, was to walk away and live her life. She'd win at BINGO and start dating again.

She went back to the closet and stood in front of it, considering her options. They were going to a dive bar for a low-key date of burgers and beer. Madeline pulled out a pair of Levi's she'd had since high school, a white t-shirt, and her black leather jacket. Comfort clothes. Old and reliable. Classic black and white. She wished the world was black and white. Or reliable. She fixed her hair so that it looked decent, but she didn't restyle it with any degree of care. She touched up her makeup and tried to smile in the mirror. *Pathetic.* She didn't want to go; she had to.

The plan was to meet up at the bar. She took a cab across the river and got there early. She found a table and pulled out her smart phone. The temptation to reread Ewan's text was there—to relive the moment before she knew what she knew about him. Even though she decided she wasn't going to jump into a monogamous relationship with him, she couldn't stop asking herself whether or not he deserved the chance he was asking for? Whether or not she should wait for him.

No. She was not about to fall in love with a guy who was just like all the others. She wanted to believe that dating all these schmucks had taught her to choose wisely when the time came, but it only made the chances of finding real love appear truly frightening. At least if she dated a schmuck, she didn't have to chance vulnerability, she didn't have to chance putting her heart out there to be crushed and stomped on over and over.

Undecided, she swiped her main menu on the phone. There was a link to her romance book of Scottish Highlander Romance. She laughed. If only she knew the ending to her own story. If only life could be so easy. She avoided Facebook and Instagram, instead clicking on Reddit to look at funny cat pictures and shitty robots. She laughed at a silly picture of a grandpa sitting on a couch with his overweight tabby next to him. Someone touched her shoulder, and she turned to see Philip behind her.

"Hey there! I'm Philip. You got here early."

She waved him to his seat. She was disappointed to see his face when all she wanted was to see was Ewan. Who was probably at home right now, packing a suitcase. Madeline gave him a bright look, a fake PR grin that stopped well before it got to her eyes. "I got here early. I thought there would be more traffic, but it was pretty clear."

Philip pulled out the chair and sat next to her. He smelled good, but it wasn't oranges and bergamot. Had she met him a week ago, she would have enjoyed kissing him later, but tonight she was almost repulsed by him. He reached out to point something out on the menu and brushed the skin on her forearm.

It took all her power not to pull back from him. *You have to kiss Philip at the Netherlands Carillon.*

Instead of trying to find the attributes about Philip that she liked, she instinctively looked for an exit.

"Is something wrong?" asked Philip. "I'm sensing that you aren't all here."

"No, no. I'm here. Just, sorry. A rough day at work, you know."

"Anything you want to talk about?"

She wanted him to be kind of an asshole so it would be easier to kiss him and ditch him. Making out with him would help her forget about Ewan.

"Just deadlines are crazy. How was your day?"

He described meeting a bunch of wealthy and famous people at the yearly fundraiser he was in charge of. She recognized a lot of the names. Normally, she would try to talk about it, at least make a contact for herself regardless of the date, but she just didn't care. Ewan was different, he didn't carry on about nonsense like name dropping.

Stop thinking about him! Madeline made herself look interested. She cocked her head and murmured, hmm, when he paused during the conversation.

The date went on, dragged on, but Phillip was nice. He wasn't Ewan, but he was nothing like the jerk Michigan lawyer guy she'd dated a week ago. They ordered dinner. He, a double bacon avocado cheeseburger with a pale ale. She, a steak salad with a Hefeweizen. He didn't try to shame her into ordering something else or otherwise show off.

If she hadn't met Ewan last weekend, she'd probably be having a great time and thinking about a fun romp in the sack later in the evening. When the salad arrived, she couldn't eat, her throat was cramped and her stomach too upset. He tried to make her laugh, told her some dumb jokes and related an anecdote about his college years. She showed him Reddit video of a cat falling over. They laughed together, but she wasn't attracted to him. After the last beer and an awkward silence, Madeline acted.

"Walk with me? I want to show you something, something special." She gave him a flirty smile. Of course he said yes.

Bile filled her stomach. Philip pulled out a fancy platinum card to pay, but Madeline insisted on paying her half. They got up and Madeline stumbled a little, tipsy from the beer and not having eaten anything that day. He put his arms around her shoulders to help steady her. She scrunched her neck in, wanting to pull away, but forced herself to lean into him. A kiss from Philip would be the best way to erase Ewan. Maybe it would even be a better kiss that would break this weird spell Ewan had over her. Winning the BINGO game would go a long way to mollify her breaking heart.

They walked down the street, directly toward the monument. As they walked, Philip's fingers brushed by hers. She knew he was trying to see if she would hold hands with him, but she ignored the signal and buttoned her jacket. Philip gave her a questioning look.

"It's colder than I thought." It wasn't true, she was practically sweating.

Madeline steered him in a way that they avoided the Dark Star park. They walked side by side. Madeline knew that if there was going to be a kiss, she had to be more personable. She tried to relax and laugh at his jokes, but her laughs came out haltingly, almost rude sounding. Madeline stretched her neck out, and took a deep breath. *Just relax. It will be okay. Get the kiss. Win BINGO. That's it.*

At the Iwo Jima memorial, Philip stopped and stepped back.

"Why did you bring me here?"

"Oh this isn't where we are stopping. There's another place. It's pretty special, I think you should see it."

"Okay. If you insist." Philip came up close to her. She could tell he was going to try and kiss her. *Too soon.*

"Come on! We're almost there!" She turned and led him across the lawn towards the Carillon. Her calves stiffened with each step. All she could think about, though, was her being here with Ewan, how they had touched each other, their mutual desire for each other feeding their passion. Here she was with another man, trying to rewrite the memory, but all she could think of was Ewan and relive the moments they'd shared together.

"I can't believe this is here," he said. "I had no idea. The Arlington cemetery is like right here."

"It's just the edge. I mean, you can't get to the main part from here."

"No, I get that, but still. This is a place no one would ever see. It's cool."

She looked hard at Phillip. He was a nice man. She would kiss him at the Netherlands Carillon and overwrite the memory of Ewan with someone new. In front of the steps, she rushed past the lions, rushed past the memory of Ewan caressing her cheeks. She practically ran up the stairs. Philip was right behind her. When she turned to face him, it scared her. Her mind had replayed the images of Ewan so vividly, that having Philip in front of her caused her to withdraw.

"You were right, this view is incredible." His hand extended to hers, but she made no move to accept. Instead, he placed his hand on the railing, in the same spot where she and Ewan had kissed. She closed her eyes wanting to erase the memories of him, but all she could think about was Ewan's hands on her. When she opened her eyes, Philip was closing in on her. He came closer, so close, she could smell the beer on his breath.

"Why did you bring me here?" His green eyes questioned her earnestly. She could tell he was about to kiss her. She leapt back.

"It's a great view, right?"

His eyes narrowed on hers. He wasn't buying it. "Yeah, it's a great view."

Madeline swallowed. There was no way she could kiss him. Not when her body was on fire for Ewan. She didn't want to be the old Madeline. She didn't want to be logical about relationships. She only wanted Ewan.

"You smell so good," Philip said, leaning in towards her body, his mouth slightly parted.

Madeline clenched her lips together and retreated back.

"I'm ... I'm so sorry Philip. Um." She scratched her temple, "I have to go." She turned and ran. She ran down the stairs, ran across the lawn, ran past the cold metal figures hoisting the flag. But she wasn't running away from Phillip as much as she was running toward her heart. The leaden weight holding her all day shifted into a senseless, illogical hope.

BACK IN HER APARTMENT, she stripped off her clothes and went into her bedroom. She was different. She had changed. There was now a before and an after. She didn't know exactly what Ewan had done to her, why he had such a hold over her. Maybe it was the way he touched her, the way he talked to her. She tried to ruminate all the different possibilities to pinpoint why she had changed so brutally and quickly. There was no way she would win BINGO or ever play a game like that again. There was no way she could even be with another man.

She was his. And she didn't care what Aundrea had told her. Her gut told her that Ewan would tell her what really happened between him and Deirdre. And she would believe him.

She laid on the bed. Her hand cupped a breast and lifted it up. With two fingers, she squeezed her nipple. With her other hand, she brushed the palm over the top of the nipple, the same palm he had caressed in the Hamptons. Her nipple swelled, trying to meet her, aching for a vigorous release. Instead, she teased her body imagining the lightness of his touch like that of his kiss on her palm--where fate met her heart.

Her clit throbbed with need. She slipped her finger between her wet lips, searching for the swollen nut. She circled it with her finger and pinched. The brief release was not enough. She needed more. She rummaged through her dresser drawer for her vibrator. The machine was German. It looked like a piece of art and nothing like a penis. She spread her legs wide and glided it into her. With her eyes closed, she pictured Ewan entering her, taking her. She belonged to him. Her back arched and she pressed the vibrator into her deeper. She wished the weight of him was on her. She wished she could lick his chest and taste his saltiness. Her body responded, and she started to rock her hips, driving it deeper and deeper inside of her.

The relentless swirling and twisting inside of her

and the rhythmic dance on her clit prepared her body for release, but thinking of Ewan took her over the edge. Instead of feeling sated though, her body was empty and unfulfilled. Instead of a calm resolution, she was more confused than ever.

Chapter 16

Friday morning. Ewan would be on an airplane headed for Central America. He would be back in eight days. The deadline for the BINGO game was five pm that evening. She could probably even check in the kiss she had with Ewan. Technically, it had happened where it was supposed to. She could still get herself a kiss, but caring about the deadline was an echo of who she used to be.

Madeline was not going to be the winner, and the knowledge left her unsure of herself. Her whole life, she had always been first place, landed the shot, or won the game, but not anymore. She wanted to go to Vegas, but she had been unable to win at BINGO. She didn't want to win for the sake of winning.

At the office, her internal negativity picked up speed. Chloe avoided her. Katherine was too busy to give her the time of day. Eleanor treated her like a stupid child after she accidentally downloaded a virus. Opal yelled at her for being fifteen minutes late to a meeting. The day could just not get any worse. At least her deliverables were completed, so she had the evening free.

It was the first Friday night in years that she had no plans to go out. At three thirty, Madeline stared at her computer. She could get a start on her next projects, but she had no enthusiasm. She clicked an email open, but was so tired from the afternoon drag, she almost fell asleep reading it. Instead of trying to work, Madeline decided to email her brother-in-law Dave to find out his side of Ewan's story. If she couldn't date anyone, she owed him the respect of gathering information to formulate her final decision. She couldn't just ghost him like all the others.

Once the email was finished, she had to decide whether to get coffee and power through the afternoon or just go home and get a fresh start for Monday. Someone from the team would be headed to Vegas, so things would be slow at the office. Next week, the secret meeting would be happening, so she'd have to be on call to provide any data and statistics, but for the most part, that research was already done and would be in the BINGO winner's hands.

She hadn't lost any competition in a while, and the

fact made her grumpy even though she knew it was the right decision. Madeline gathered her things and put them in her leather briefcase. She felt the weekend thrill go through her veins. Even though she had canceled all her plans, she was excited to be leaving the office. She headed out and walked down the hall, her heels clicking along. There was another text notification on her phone. She assumed it was going to be an invite to some party, but was shocked when she saw the name.

Ewan.

Nothing else mattered to her in that moment and she stopped in the middle of the hallway. People grunted at her in disapproval as they swerved to avoid her, their complaints floating past her. The only thing she cared about was the message on her phone.

Ewan: I know about this BINGO game. We have to talk as soon as I'm back.

The background disappeared, and she could barely breathe. *Oh shit.* Had she been alone in her apartment, she would have let herself crumple to the floor, but she was in a packed hallway of the Congressional building, surrounded by acquaintances and co-workers. The lump in her throat was back. True, he might have been a player in his day, but she had been playing a game too.

Madeline wanted to talk to someone, but she

didn't have any real friends to turn to, only party buddies. The hell if she was going to call her sister. Her mom was not one for relationship advice, she was all about the end game. Her dad? Maybe. He was the only one she was willing to talk to, who knew her but would also give impartial advice.

There was a truth she had to face, a reality that she didn't want to think about. Her own actions and her own lifestyle was not conducive to love or even friendship. Could she change the way she lived her life, the people she chose to surround herself with? Did she want to take a chance with Ewan? Or did she want to go back to the old Madeline who didn't have a care in the world?

The truth was she had never had a man in her life who wanted her, who had treated her with consideration, or who believed that she was meant for him. Past lovers always wanted something else. Ewan wanted her. *But what did she want?* She gathered her composure, or whatever was left of it, and walked out of the building.

Chapter 17

*E*ight days passed. Ewan was coming back sometime today, and Madeline was not ready to leave the safe haven of her bed. He hadn't texted her back for four whole days, and they hadn't discussed their relationship. She groaned, of course it was better to wait so they could talk face to face. But she had already waited eight long days, and patience was not her forte. *What if he planned to ghost me?* No. He wouldn't do that, would he?

Usually on a Saturday morning, by 10:00 am she would have already gone for a run, had a cup of coffee, an egg for breakfast, and would be on her phone making plans for the weekend. Madeline had meant to meet up with her dad before Ewan got back, but as luck would have it, their schedules didn't match up. Tonight, she'd have dinner with her dad and then hit a late-night party with Jeannie. Ewan may be getting back in town today, but he hadn't done anything to set up a date or time for them to talk. Her dad and a party with Jeannie would provide her with plenty of diversion.

Still, she didn't want to get out of bed. She must be a lunatic for letting him affect her so strongly. *How did that happen?* Part of her wanted to just drop the whole thing, to ghost him first. But she wanted to see Ewan. She wanted to look into his eyes once more.

Everything is going to be alright.

The smartphone on her nightstand had no notification lights flashing. *Why hadn't he called or texted?* Maybe he lost his phone. Maybe he didn't have coverage in Guatemala. Instead, she had several emails from Dave telling her about Ewan, what he had been up to, his past with women, a picture of him playing soccer with some kids, even what he had for breakfast. The emails promised that Ewan was a good guy, that Aundrea didn't have the whole story. He apologized for telling Ewan about the BINGO game, too. Madeline scratched the back of her neck. Those two must have had an interesting conversation on their flight from Texas to Guatemala.

Apparently Deirdre's family had old money. Dave's layman version described her as a lunatic New York lawyer with too much time on her hands.

Sociopath? *Maybe.* No, he didn't have actual proof, but it wasn't the first time Deirdre had gone all nut job on a guy. He'd straighten out Aundrea and tell her everything he knew about Deirdre, he promised. The last email Dave had sent let her know they were leaving Guatemala on Saturday at 6:00 am local time. Ewan would be back Saturday afternoon. She checked the time. It was 11:30 am. *Was he home yet?*

Her text notification buzzed. It was her dad asking if she could come over early and go to the Indian grocery store with him. He wanted to practice cooking something new for her, a difficult Indian dish called Kashmiri Dum Aloo. She texted her dad back saying she'd be there by three. This was most excellent. She could focus on her dad and Kashmiri whatever instead of her miserable state. Surely the rooftop party with Jeannie would take care of the rest of the night. There was an open bar and a DJ, and the weather was supposed to be perfect.

Madeline checked the main menu of her smartphone. There were four missed calls from her sister already and one email that she had not yet responded to. She had ignored Aundrea's calls and emails since she last talked to her. Dave had sent an email requesting, more like begging, that she call her sister, that Aundrea was worried about her, that she wanted to talk. When Madeline read this, her body tensed. She wanted nothing to do with her bossy, manipulating, overbearing sister.

She looked over her texts from Ewan. After the BINGO text, he had texted again, letting her know he was in Guatemala and that everything was good. She had replied with a thumbs up emoji, not knowing what to say. Leaving the text unanswered seemed worse. A day later, the first email from Dave came.

She clicked into her email app to reread all the emails. She scrolled down and reread the first letter Dave wrote. Dave had asked Aundrea for the whole story, and so he knew that Deirdre had accused Ewan of throwing money at her for an abortion, that he supposedly said something like, 'take care of it.'

Ewan never did that. She probably made the whole thing up for attention from Aundrea. Madeline had written back asking specifics and questions. As she reread her words, her tone seemed to bounce between jaded and overprotective to resounding desperation.

After the first email with Dave, she had thought hard about Ewan, trying to gauge his character, trying to understand what she wanted. *She wanted to be smart about love.* But she didn't want to regret missing a chance with him.

Or was he just some first-class conman? She just wished she could know with certainty. She was used to having a physical opponent in front of her, to know her adversary. Frustrated by the lack of being able to actually talk to Deirdre, her sister, or Ewan, she wanted to punch something.

Maybe it didn't matter though. One night, Madeline had gone to a happy hour in order to get her mind off the situation. In the bathroom, she was fixing her lipstick when she had an aha moment. *She was being smart about love.* Her emotions might be crazy, but she was evaluating what she knew and making a somewhat rational attempt to make a decision about Ewan. She honed in on the message: Be smart about love.

She knew Ewan, she had seen his Instagram photos, she knew he would protect her, the way he did with Corbin, the way he held her hand. *He believed they were meant to be together. The way he looked at her.* She knew the kind of man he was, the kind of man he was to her, and everything else was hearsay.

She trusted Dave's version of Ewan. He wouldn't email her from Guatemala if he didn't trust and like Ewan. And Dave was her brother-in-law, he was on her side. And honestly, even though she was still angry about it, Aundrea was looking out for her too. She remembered her dad's advice. *Use your gut.* She closed her eyes and focused on her body.

Inside her, deep in her belly, she knew Ewan was a good man. She knew he was right for her. She would wait for him. With her heart about to pound out of her chest, she wrote and sent the text back to Ewan.

Madeline: I'm waiting for you.

She pulled the covers up over her head and wrapped her arms and legs around a king size pillow, hugging it tightly. At least for a little bit she could pretend ignorance of the whole debacle and snuggled in where the warmth and comfort provided a mini oasis.

By 1:00 PM, she forced herself to get up. It would be too easy to feel sorry for herself, to stay in pajamas all day. But if she indulged her dejection, she had learned it was harder to bounce back. There was no use sitting around feeling pathetic and useless. She rolled herself out of bed and into the shower. Afterwards, she dried off and put on a pair of clean yoga pants. She placed her rooftop party outfit into a garment bag along with the shoes. Her dad planned to cook Indian, she didn't want the smell of curry to permeate her outfit.

At his apartment, she hung her garment bag up in the closet. He had a glass of wine ready for her in the kitchen, and she took a long drink. The liquid soothed her throat and settled her stomach.

"I'm not going to make the Indian dish. It requires

a pressure cooker. I didn't want to buy one to make a single dish."

"Okay." She wanted to care, but she couldn't quite get out of her funk. She filled up the glass of wine and stared off in the distance. "Whatever."

"You know me and pressure-cookers," he said attempting to lighten the situation. "Okay. Somebody is in a bad mood. I'm going to make butternut squash raviolis instead. With a sweet sage creamy béchamel. It's a trifle easier. I'm excited to experiment with some new flavors."

"Daddy, are you going to divorce Mom?"

He paused momentarily and straightened his shoulders. He finished putting the wine into the fridge and turned to her. "That's pretty direct. Where did that come from?"

"How did you know when you met her?"

"That kind of question..." He stopped short, uncrossed his arms and shrugged, his forehead wrinkling in deep lines. "It's hard to say exactly what it was. I just knew. Back then, we were both ambitious kids, we wanted to change the world."

"That's it? You give me some bullshit story? A cliché too."

"But that's the way it happens. It just happens. When you fall in love, it feels like this is the first time you've ever felt love, the first time anyone ever made sense. For me, I had this drive to succeed. My plan was to work hard, to write my name and place in this world. She wanted to do the same. We fit."

"So that's it? You just shared the same goal. Why didn't you marry the CEO then?"

"Okay Madeline, simmer down." He scratched his chin. "I don't know how better to explain it to you. One day, you wake up, and you know that whatever it is you've been looking for your whole life is somehow contained in this person. That they are tailored specifically for you. You just *know* this person. And I don't mean the color of their hair or how they smile, but you have found something important and ancient."

"That sounds like a bad romance."

"Come on now. You asked me. I'm telling you how I felt." Louis added milk to the sauce. "I'm telling you something that is hard for me to say. I don't like that mumbo jumbo either. I'm at heart, a programmer. I'm a facts and logic guy. But love? Makes you think you're the first person to notice how blue the sky is."

Madeline took a firm hold of her wine stem. She lifted it up with precision and took a sip. She wanted her life to be a logic and facts kind of life, including love. She had always explained away love, telling herself that it was a series of chemicals the brain produced. Serotonin. Oxytocin. Dopamine. She gave love another whirl in college. She trusted him, and he decided to stick his penis in another woman. Then a string of unsuccessful dating followed, all of them wanted to fuck her, then fuck her over, but no one wanted her. Love? No thank you.

But then there was Ewan. She felt like she had known him her whole life, that they were meant to be. Madeline lowered her eyes.

"I know Dad. You're right." Ewan had clearly shown in not only words but actions that he wanted them to be together, but she still didn't know, she wasn't sure if she could trust *feelings*.

Could she be happy being alone the rest of her life? All she needed was memories and a vibrator. And besides, she had already completed a milestone in her life: it is better to have loved and lost, than to never have loved at all. *Check.*

"Love at first sight then?" Madeline asked sarcastically. "Why do you want to divorce her then? Did your feelings go away?"

The timer beeped. He opened the oven and pulled out a foil covered butternut squash and placed it on a trivet.

"No," he said quietly, intent on the bowl in front of him. "I guess it happened over time, but it didn't feel that way. One day, I woke up and wanted more than the tech life. I didn't want to work a hundred hours a week. That kind of adrenaline fueled work didn't appeal to me anymore."

He looked up to meet her eyes. "I still want to be with your Mom. Marriage is hard. I still love her, and now it's deeper because we've had kids and worked through a lot of hard times. But it doesn't change the fact that we both have grown up. And apart. We are different. I love going out to see my vines and letting the dirt run through my fingers. I can't go back to San Francisco. We made it work for a long time, but now, we hardly see each other. What's the point? I guess I want a clean break."

"Is there someone else?"

"Another woman? No. Unless you count my grapes." He retrieved a spoon from one of the drawers and scooped the cooked squash out of its shell.

"The love is starting to fade?" Madeline asked. She had started the sentence with an edge, but by the last word, she had a more sympathetic tone.

"If I am going to be married, I want to spend actual time with that person."

"Why not go back to the City?" she asked, but already knowing the answer. "Wouldn't it be worth it to save your marriage?"

"I guess I could, but the end result would still be divorce. I wouldn't be happy in the City for more than a couple of days. I can't go back. That life..." He paused for a moment to clean his glasses off. "That life in San Francisco isn't me. That life has a cost and I don't want to pay it. I made my money, I made my name. I'm satisfied. I'll always love your mom, but I don't think she wants to be with me."

"Why don't you let her make that decision?"

"Your mom can't let anything fail, ever. I thought that if I did it, if I left her, it'd be easier for her."

She was just like her mom, afraid of failure. Her stomach twisted and lurched. She had no idea what to do with this or how to change it.

"A mercy divorce?" she asked, unwilling to let it go.

"Madeline, this isn't easy for me." Louis set the pot down on the stove and it clattered. Béchamel sauce splattered onto the counter. "I want to be with your mom. She says she wants to be with me. I just don't know if she really wants that or if she's afraid to admit we've failed. She has agreed to take an extended leave from San Francisco and help me start the restaurant. So, that will be the final test, I guess." He turned the gas stove on and a flame burst out under the pan. "But ... I don't know. Will she like being out of her element?" He added olive oil to the pan and slid the chopped onions in. "Why are you asking? Is something going on with you? Aundrea must have called five times this last week, asking if I'd seen you, to tell you to call her."

"Oh Aundrea," Madeline sighed. She heard her text notification beep. "It's complicated."

"Seems like I'm not the only one here with problems."

Madeline made a face at him, a half smirk, half smile. She went to retrieve her phone, which she had left in her purse. Opening the screen, she saw it was from Ewan.

Ewan: I'm back. I want to see you. Tomorrow brunch?

Her heart pounded in her ears. Past the thunderous roar and the immediate excitement that welled up in her chest, she almost dropped the phone. He was back in town. He *did* want to see her. She had so many questions for him, but couldn't imagine how the conversation would go. She clutched her pendant, the one her mom gave her of a fencer in a lunge move, and ran it back and forth against the chain. *Slow down Asher. You need to be smart, don't be an emotional basket case.*

Madeline: Yes. Where?

Ewan: I'll pick you up at 10. Little diner in Crystal City.

Madeline returned to the kitchen. A smile now

covered her face where just a few minutes ago she had been sullen and snappy with her dad.

"Wow. There's an about face if I ever saw one."

Madeline looked up in surprise; it was a quick change. She didn't like being at the mercy of her feelings and wanted to change the subject. "What else are you going to add to the butternut? Rosemary might be nice."

"It will clash with the sage. You know, I have too many kinds of food that I like. Who knows what will go on the menu."

Madeline started to think about what she would wear for brunch. Should she wear her sexy underwear? Was the brunch going to end up at Ewan's apartment?

"Earth to Madeline! Hey! I'm over here. You aren't getting out of it that easy. Tell me what's going on with Aundrea."

Madeline paused, wondering where to start. She wasn't sure if she wanted to tell her dad anything about Ewan, especially since they knew each other, and Madeline didn't want to jeopardize any business relationship the two of them might have. She needed his advice, and more importantly, she trusted him.

"Alright. Here it is..." Madeline related the story of how she met Ewan in the Hampton's, how he had stood up for her, and how Aundrea had told her to keep away from him. She told him about their fantastic date just before Ewan left for Guatemala. Then, she told him how Aundrea informed her of Deirdre's pregnancy story and Ewan's gross denial of it.

"But, Dad," she said, "According to Dave's email, the pregnancy story was made up by some nut-job. It's all so crazy-sounding, isn't it?

Madeline took a breath of air. Now Ewan wanted to meet for brunch. Living the story in her mind was one thing—all the little nuances were easy enough to maneuver around. But, relating all of it to another person reignited the emotional roller coaster she had been on.

"That's quite a story. Hmmmm..." He put a pot of water on the stove and turned the burner on a high flame. "I'm still thinking about all that." Then, he added the remaining ingredients to a bowl to make the dough for the ravioli. Madeline considered telling him about the BINGO game, that she had been playing a kissing game when she met Ewan, but he turned the mixer on. She decided it was better not to. He didn't need to know about the game, and she was already facing up to her past. He got out a French rolling pin and plopped the dough from the mixing bowl, kneading it gradually to a ball.

"I know I'm supposed to use a pasta machine, but I didn't have one of those either." He placed his hands on his hips and looked around the kitchen. "Jeez, these kitchen tools are killing me."

He rolled out the dough. The back and forth was oddly soothing. Madeline found the radio and turned it on to a classical station and low volume. He didn't seem to notice and kept rolling away.

"Aw crap," he said, setting the pin down "I was supposed to let the dough rest before rolling it out."

"Is it ruined?"

"I don't think so, but, well, we are where we are. I'm not starting over." He sprinkled flour over the dough. With a small ice cream scoop, he plopped drops of the squash filling onto the dough, folded it over, and cut out squares. He dusted the raw ravioli, flipped them over.

"Work with what you have," he said holding up a textured bowl that he used to crimp the edges.

Madeline pulled away the unused dough and rolled the smaller pieces into a big one.

"First, I want to talk about your sister," he said. The water bubbled in the pot. He slid the spatula under and dropped two at a time into the boiling liquid.

"I love Andrea. You know that." He scooped two more ravioli's up and slipped them into the water. "I know she helped to raise you. Mom and I were gone a lot. Not fair to her, but that was on us. Rosa was there for you, but it wasn't the same. Andrea, sorry Aundrea, was your best friend for a lot of years. Maybe more like a mom than a sister. You two have a very long and complicated past."

Madeline swallowed hard. She pushed back the swelling of emotions that threatened to overwhelm her, not to avoid them, but so that she could hear what her dad had to say. He scooped up two more raviolis and slid them into the water.

"She loves you and is very protective." He turned down the heat of the stove. "But, you are both adults. You're almost twenty-eight and she's what, thirty? Your relationship is changing, and that can be painful."

"She doesn't need to be sticking her nose in my business. She always does that. She could have ruined everything for Ewan and me. I don't know if it can be fixed."

"Honey, slow down." He set the timer for the raviolis. "I know Aundrea was looking out for your best interest. She doesn't want to see you hurt."

Madeline slumped into her seat. She rubbed her temples and pushed back her hair. "She has to stop bossing me around."

"You have to tell her this. You've proved to be a very capable adult. Aundrea is watching out for her little sister, and you would do the same for her. If you had heard Dave was a cheating jerk, you'd be the first to tell her."

"I know," she said, the anger subsiding. "You're right."

"Just remember who she really is and why she is saying what she's saying." He pulled out a large bowl from the fridge. "I already made the salad this morning, I got bored. Did you want another glass of wine?"

"No thanks. If I keep going at this rate, I'll be drunk before the rooftop party."

"Don't do that." He took the raviolis off the stove. He drained the liquid and dumped them into a serving bowl. In the same pan, he added the sauce and placed it on the stove.

"Now, let's talk about Ewan." A wooden spoon was on the counter top and Madeline slid it towards her dad. He picked it up and stirred.

"Ewan is more complicated to advise on, only because I've met him the once so I don't know that much. But I can tell you what I've learned about people from being a CIO."

Madeline nodded at him, quiet.

"I know you haven't had the best boyfriends in the past. And I know that your mom and I are probably not the best example of a healthy relationship. But what I do know is this..." He stopped stirring and pointed the spoon at her, not caring that he dripped béchamel everywhere. "If he is texting you after all this drama? If he asked Dave to send you an email to verify his innocence, which I believe he did..." She nodded to let him know she was listening. "Well, then you should try. He seems to be a good man. I would at least find out what's going on from the horse's mouth. At the very least, he deserves an answer from you."

"I want to run away and pretend it never happened. I wish it wasn't so hard. Isn't love supposed to be easy?"

"I think the kids call it *adulting* now. He seems to really like you. If he didn't care about you, he wouldn't have contacted you."

Madeline chuckled. It was one thing to hear someone like Chloe or Cheyenne say 'adulting', but it was funny to hear it come out of her dad's mouth. Her shoulders felt lighter, the unfulfilled ache of not having cried lifted from her as well.

"It wasn't what you would call a conversation. He asked me to wait for him, until he got back. So we could talk."

He got up from his chair and went back into the kitchen. He took the pot off the stove. "Did you wait?"

Madeline opened the cabinet doors and retrieved the dishes. "I tried to go on a date with someone else. I mean, well, I left in the middle of it. The thought of being with someone else ..."

"Well. There you have it. I don't think Ewan wants to hurt you. I mean, he isn't trying to deceive you. You should see him again."

"He just sent me a text. We're meeting tomorrow for brunch."

"Good. That'll be good. Then you'll know. Besides, maybe you are making this way bigger than it is. If you don't like him, don't date him. It's simple." He took another bite of his food. "Trust your gut sweetheart. And eat some of my food before it gets cold."

"Then I'll know, right? When I see him tomorrow? I'll trust my gut."

"That's it sweetheart. Trust your gut. Now...if you ever do want to run away, I am looking for a wedding planner at the winery. You'd be perfect."

Madeline got up from her spot and approached her dad. She kissed him squarely on the cheek. "Thanks Daddy. I needed to hear that."

"You're my baby. I'd do anything for you, you know that. Now sit down, eat, and tell me how delicious my raviolis are."

$\mathcal{M}$adeline arrived at a nondescript building constructed with white cement and wondered if this rooftop party would be worth it. She almost canceled with her girlfriend Jeannie, but after dinner and a good talk with her dad, her whole mood had shifted. She was glad to be out in public, not feeling sad, or upset, or mad at her sister. She wanted to have fun, enjoy a couple drinks with her friends, have some interesting conversation, and listen to good music. She was in for a treat as the guys from the Thievery Corporation would be at the DJ helm.

The lobby was crammed with party goers. The elevator door dinged, and they fit comfortably into a functional elevator straight to the rooftop. There was no reason for the party, Jeannie had told her, aside from a wealthy lawyer who wanted to have fun. They stepped out into a place that was beautifully decorated, completely opposite of the stark lobby and functional elevator. White twinkle-lights were strung from wooden poles. Seven-foot tall heaters kept the air warm. Funky music played in the background. She let the mood sway her shoulders.

The rooftop had no view of the monuments, being too far away, but the skyline was dotted with cranes and the general dim of city light. There were lounge chairs and Adirondacks, giving the place a beachy feel which reminded her of the party at the Hamptons. Tomorrow she'd have brunch with Ewan. Tomorrow she'd know. A comfortable feeling settled over her belly.

"Madeline!" Jeannie waved at her cheerfully from across the room. She was eager to see her friend after missing her at last week's PRSA meeting. They had met five years before when they kept running into each other on the party circuit. They had hit it off and subsequently invited each other to more parties. Madeline liked the sassy girl from the Midwest.

"This party is turning out to be more European than American," she said. "And I have to say, I love the cheek kisses from hot men. They never did that in Kansas when I was growing up."

Madeline laughed. She did love Jeannie's humor.

Salt of the earth. Jeannie had started off as a secretary for the National Geographic Association, but started to submit her work and was now a published travel author, sometimes photographer if they needed. She was one of the few people in DC who knew everybody and all the circulating rumors, but somehow never involved herself. She had joined the PRSA to find new acquaintances and learn how to better present her work. She was a sweetheart.

"Who else is here?" asked Madeline, swooping her view around the patio to see if she recognized anyone. And there he was. In khaki pants and a printed shirt. He was tan. She could see the color of his brilliant blue eyes even from where she stood.

Everything stopped for her, the music faded into oblivion. The partygoers diminished. She wasn't ready to see him tonight. She felt like she was still recuperating from the last eight days and gathering energy for her date tomorrow. She'd be better prepared tomorrow.

"Who are you looking ... Oh my God! Madeline," Jeannie said grasping her elbow, leaning in close, "do you know who that is?"

She nodded, but said nothing.

"You know that is Ewan Shannon, right?" Jeannie said his name as if he was a celebrity or something. When Madeline stared blankly back at her and shook her head, Jeannie sighed. "I told you about this…"

Madeline was sure her face took on a cartoonish response. "Ewan? What did you tell me about Ewan?"

"I'm sure I told you. You know, about the guy who was dumped at the altar? The huge society blowout? It was so shocking."

Madeline shook her head. It was possible that Jeannie had told her about it, but she had either forgotten or not really been listening. Jeannie was a talker, and sometimes she meandered. A lot.

"I was invited to this wedding last year, maybe a year and a half ago, in Chevy Chase. My ex-boyfriend knew the bride to be in college, she was one of his roommates. Ewan used to be a hedge fund manager. He was running some environmental groups. And she was the heir to someone who invented a famous cleaning product. A trust fund baby girl."

Madeline couldn't speak. She couldn't take her eyes off him. He was here. Talking to another person as if he had not a care in the world.

Jeannie had turned to look at Ewan too. "He is good looking, isn't he? Babe might be a better word. Hot is sufficient I suppose. I wouldn't kick him out of bed for all the spilled crumbs in the world."

"So what happened?" asked Madeline, putting a hand on Jeannie's shoulder. "At the wedding."

"Oh yes..." Jeannie returned her gaze to Madeline. "Well, I don't know the whole story, I mean, the story behind the story, but anyway, there he is at the altar. He's wearing this great tuxedo. You can tell he's nervous, right? He seems excited to be getting married though, not nervous I don't want to do this nervous. Just regular getting married today nervous."

Madeline was losing all patience with her friend. "Jeannie!"

"Okay, just wanting to tell you the buildup, calm down missy." She took another sip of her wine. Just when Madeline thought she would explode, Jeannie started again. "Then the music started. Bum bum ba bum ... Everyone stood up and looking down the aisle, waiting for her to appear, waiting for the big moment. I mean her dad didn't even know. He looked mortified at the entrance of that church."

"She never showed up?"

"That's right. I guess she got in a cab and left while no one was looking."

"A cab?"

"Hi there," said a deep voice. Not just any deep voice. Ewan's deep voice.

She had been so engrossed in Jeannie's story she hadn't noticed he'd moved. Madeline's eyes flew open. She could smell him already and that alone sent her body aflame. She wanted so badly to turn around without abandon and give him the biggest hug she had ever given anyone, but she stood stone still.

"Ewan," said Jeannie. "It's good to see you here. I want to introduce you to ..."

"Madeline."

"Yes. Oh wow. You two already know each other? This is awkward." Jeannie looked at Madeline and nodded towards Ewan, trying to clue her in that there was obviously a man who stood behind her. Madeline swallowed the lump in her throat. She wasn't sure if her body would run madly, or if she would cry or laugh manically, so she turned slowly. When she looked into his blue eyes of sky, she couldn't help but smile. All the doubt she felt for the last eight days disappeared. She was thankful that she hadn't won BINGO. She was beyond ecstatic that the date with Philip went to complete crap.

"Hi Ewan. It's good to see you."

"Same." He stepped back and looked at Jeannie. "I don't want to intrude here." He switched his focus back to Madeline. "Come find me when you're done."

Madeline couldn't be sure if she had even responded. Had she stood there blinking mutely at him? Had she nodded? With a deep breath, she watched as Ewan Shannon, the man himself, walked towards his friends on the other side of the rooftop. Of all the places in all the world, and he shows up at this party on this night. Well if that wasn't fate, she wasn't sure what was.

"You KNOW Ewan? How in the ... what a freaking small world. Sweet cheeks, you have to tell me everything."

She was still trying to catch her breath let alone speak.

"I met him in New York two weeks ago. My sister wanted me to visit, and she dragged me to this boring fundraiser, and there he was. Raising money for kids in Guatemala."

"Guatemala, huh? I heard that he took off after the wedding. Quit his job, sold all his things. He really loved her you know. Then for her to just not show up. Ugh. I can't even imagine how terrible that would be."

"To be dumped in front of everyone like that? She didn't even have the guts to say anything to him, she left... like he was nothing." The weight of the pain he had been through made her sad and she felt twinges of protectiveness. "Who does that?"

"At least have some balls to talk to him before dumping him at the altar. Fast forward eighteen months and Ewan Shannon wants to talk to you. He looked pretty serious."

"It's a long story Jeannie." Madeline stopped and looked over the edge of the fenced balcony. "Not long, but complicated."

"I have time."

Jeannie was asking because she cared, not just trying to get some story out of her. She knew she could trust Jeannie, but she didn't want to do that to Ewan. She didn't want to add any details to the misery of his narrative, being left at the altar. No matter what happened, the last thing she wanted to do was hurt him. "Let's meet later this week for lunch okay? I'd love to see you again."

"You're not going to tell me?"

"No."

"Hey Jeannie!" A pretty blonde woman glided up to her and kissed her on the cheek. "How are you?"

Before Jeannie could respond to the newcomer, Madeline touched her forearm and pointed to the bar. "Do you want another drink?"

Jeannie nodded and turned her attention to her other friend. Madeline walked over to the open bar decorated nicely with bright triangle flags reminiscent of those on a sailing ship. She weaved through a group of people and could hear different accents drift by. At the bar, she ordered a glass of wine. When the bartender handed her two glasses of chardonnay, she considered her dad's offer. She could quit this DC party world and go to California. There, she'd get a chance to be with her dad, to develop a relationship in a way that she had always longed for as a kid.

"Allo miz," said a man's voice.

Madeline knew without looking that the greeting was directed to her.

"You enjoy the evening, no?"

"It's a nice night." She tossed him a dismissive smile. Madeline tried to find Jeannie in the midst of the crowd with the plan of ditching this Italian.

"Is a beautiful night too, no?" he asked.

The word reminded her of Ewan, the way he called her beautiful. She turned to look at him. Truth be told, he was a handsome Italian, but he had a steely look of determination that reminded her of a used car salesman. She refrained from letting out an exasperated sigh. She wouldn't be rude unless he went from small talk to persistent flirt.

"It is a beautiful night," she said, looking through the crowd for Jeannie and hoping to see Ewan.

He took this as a positive sign and stepped in closer, putting his arm around her shoulders. "We look at the stars together then, no?"

Madeline didn't want him touching her. She tried to twist her way out of his arms but he held on. "Madam, you are like a goldfish, very wiggle-wiggle. You want to come somewhere with me?"

"No."

"Hey Gino, you know Madeline?"

The Italian's arm retracted. Madeline turned to find herself looking at Ewan.

"No, we meet just now. I was showing her the beautiful stars," he said. "*Scusami*, are you two?" He waved his hand back and forth between Madeline and Ewan.

Madeline chuckled quietly. Ewan had a face that could win high stakes poker games; his expression was one-hundred percent neutral.

"It's a great night out, I have to agree. The stars are beautiful, Madeline. Might I have the honor to escort you back to Jeannie?" He held his hand out for her, inviting her to go with him.

The way he said beautiful made her weak in the knees. He said it the same way he had at the Netherlands Carillon. The way he had said it to her in bed. She bit the side of her lip.

"I would love that. Thank you Ewan." With two glasses of wine in her hand, she couldn't take his hand. Stepping in close, she gave him a kiss on the cheek instead. They walked through the crowd. The air on her skin was warm, and yet goosebumps prickled her flesh.

After they left the Italian, Madeline said, "You're always saving me Ewan, what's up with that?"

"It's what I have to do," he said with a lop-sided grin, half smile, half guarded. "Will you leave with me, instead? Right now?" A wrinkle appeared between his eyebrows and his lips tightened. He took the glasses of wine from her and set them on a nearby table. Then, he gathered her hands, looked at them carefully and rubbed the center of her palm. "It's killing me to be here pretending everything is okay."

Acting more on instinct than she did logic, she squeezed his hand, her fingers wrapped around his. She found Jeannie in the crowd again, but decided to text her goodbye rather than try to explain anything right now. What words would she use? They were all stuck in her swelling, hope-filled heart. They walked together to the elevator hand in hand.

Chapter 19

In the middle of the night, Ewan and Madeline rode in a cab across the 14th street bridge. A full moon was out, blooming along the horizon. He sat next to her, holding her hand still, tracing a finger along the lines of her palm. A curious calm washed over her. In spite of her own past and Ewan's as well, she knew everything would be alright. She felt that surety, in her bones, in the way the dark water lapped against the shore of the Potomac, in the way he touched her ever so gentle and ever so firm.

Nearly every moment of the cab ride home was locked into her memory. The sound of vehicles passing them on the GW Parkway. The lights of the city, on the bridge, in the distance. She noted the faint twinkling of stars. Being with the man she loved, in this vehicle, on the way to whatever was about to happen had no bearing to that of any fairy tale she knew. But perhaps a fairy tale is the only way to describe that secret passageway so many lovers have traveled. The passage of before and after. This very route, this ordinary cab ride was one that would lead to a new kingdom, a new land, a faraway place she had never been to before.

Neither of them spoke the entire way. They glanced at each other, they smiled, but nothing was said. Ewan paid the driver. She let his hand go, and got out, and met him at the door. Once he caught up, he took her hand again. The last time they stood at the entrance to his lobby, they had walked back from the Netherlands Carillon. It seemed then, there was an air of lightness, a sense of innocence. Tonight was much more somber.

She wondered what would happen next. Madeline wasn't afraid as much as she was hopeful. Excited. She didn't want to go back to being the old Madeline. She just wasn't sure how they would forge ahead. The old Madeline would have had a conversation like this already mapped out in her head. He would say this. She would say that. And that would be that. But not tonight.

He unlocked the door and stood aside, welcoming her in with a swoop of his arm. She entered of her own volition. She turned and held out her hand. Ewan took it, and they walked in together. He found a bottle of wine in the fridge and poured two glasses of wine, handing one to her.

"You want to sit down?"

Madeline sat on the bar stool. Her back was straight. Her eyes centered on his.

"First, I want to tell you that I am going to be honest. You can ask me anything at all, anything about Guatemala, anything about Deirdre, and anything about my ex. But first, I have a question..." He settled his hands flat against the countertop. "Was I one of your BINGO conquests?" He squared his shoulders. "Did you use me for your game?"

"No." Madeline kept eye contact with him. "I could have, but ... I chose not to. I didn't want to do that to you."

"Did you wait for me?"

"I went on a date, but I couldn't ... I left him in the middle of ... I felt bad leaving him but ... I spent an hour with him and nothing happened. All I could think about was you," she said, trying to find the words to explain herself.

Ewan came around the island and stood close to her, but didn't touch her. "I understand."

"So...I heard about you and..." Madeline didn't know the other woman's name. "Heard about you being left at the altar?"

He sat in front of her, their legs naturally settled between one other like a basket weave. "Carrie. Her name is Carrie. We're friends now. Not really friends, but at least we don't hate each other."

"What happened?"

"She couldn't bring herself to tell me that she didn't want to get married. Felt like she was in too deep, and she was scared to tell me. Then, she just walked out. Grabbed a cab. Like that. She was gone."

"Jeannie tells me you left for Guatemala after that."

"Yeah. I tried to drown my sorrows in other women, but that didn't work out so well. Then, I came back to the states. I really loved Carrie, it was hard for me. When Bunny offered me a job as the fundraiser for the foundation, I felt like I found some purpose. The sun seemed a little brighter. The sadness started to fade."

"In high school, a guy broke my heart. Told everyone I had slept with him, and he didn't want anything to do with me. I know it was a long time ago, but it shook the wind out of me Then I dated again in college. He cheated on me. Since then, it's just been a series of bad fizzled romances. Feeling used." She acknowledged his murmurs of indignation. "It doesn't sound that bad, I know, but I just wanted so badly to meet the right guy and it never happened. Trying to stay hopeful that I'd meet a guy after five years of dating, was well, hard."

"I know the feeling," he said, "But ..." he lifted his hands and placed his palm against her neck, his thumb caressed her chin, and his fingers warming the back of her neck. "I know you. There's something about you that I just, that I *know*."

"Who was Deirdre?" she asked, her voice catching in her throat. She leaned away from him, and placed his hand in her lap.

"She was a woman I dated. One of New York's finest defense attorneys, she was a hard hitter and smart as hell. When it finally dawned on me that she wasn't the one, I broke up with her. Anyway, Deirdre told me she was pregnant. When she did, I didn't want to marry her. In all honesty, I wasn't ready to be a father. But I told her we could co-parent." He said, picking up her hand in his and she accepted his touch. "I wanted her to take a paternity test. All of a sudden, she was gone. I never saw her again."

Madeline lifted her chin to gauge his sincerity.

"I have all her emails if you want to see them."

"I trust you Ewan." Adrenaline raced into her heart, it started thumping against her ribs, thinking it might burst apart. She had said it out loud, without thinking about it. Her gut had said it for her.

"I thought about it hard when I was in

Guatemala and the truth is, I don't care about your past. The BINGO game I mean. I was hurt when I first found out." He looked her in the eye. "But I figured there was a reason. I couldn't stop thinking about you."

"I just wanted to win, that was all. I guess it was stupid." She flexed her toes and stared at the top of her feet.

Ewan brought her hands up to his mouth and kissed her fingers. "It doesn't matter, unless you plan on continuing to play."

"No I don't want to. I mean, it was over last week. I lost." She shrugged. She didn't want to talk about Vegas.

"Are you done playing games?"

Madeline swallowed and found that the lump in her throat was no longer there. She was done playing games and nodded emphatically. "I am absolutely, completely, forever done."

"What I want you to know now," he said between kisses down her arm, "is that ... you ... are my missing piece." He paused the kisses and brought his head up to meet her gaze. Madeline could have sworn that a cool breeze had come into the kitchen because she had a chill. Ewan continued kissing her lightly and returned to her shoulder. She lifted her chin again, and he rubbed the stubble of his beard against her neck.

She closed her eyes wanting to remember every sensation of this moment.

He whispered in her ear, "Come with me."

This was it. This was the edge of her precipice. She could still say no, she could still run out and try to be her old self. She bit her lip, then smiled with confidence, a gesture that was reflective, one that said goodbye to the old Madeline. The switch had already turned, she only had to see the light.

She met his mouth. He parted her lips with his tongue, his kisses giving the answers to questions she had deep inside of her. His hands encircled her, he pressed her to him, and she put her arms around his neck.

He led her out of the kitchen, through the living room, down the hall. The bathroom light was on and drops of water were on the tile. They continued to his bedroom.

Ewan lit a couple of candles that decorated his room. He turned on his iPod, and Mayan folk music played. He opened his window. A soft breeze floated his curtains. She stood on the opposite side of the bed from him and unbuttoned her shirt. It drifted to the ground. She could have sworn fairies came to take it away from her. Her nipples were hard under the silky cup of her bra, but she left it on.

"Beautiful. I'll never get tired of looking at you." He took off his shirt and dropped it.

She took off her pants, pushing the material over her hips, letting it glide over her. They fell into a heap at her feet. She left her underwear on, ocean blue, to match the color of his eyes. He pulled down his jeans until they too were at his feet. His boxers barely covered his erect penis, aiming for her once again, knowing what it wanted.

He walked around the bed and kissed her, his tongue matching her lunge and retreat. He lifted the strap of her bra and let it fall over her shoulder, and then he did the same with the other strap. The curve of her breast was the only thing holding up the bra. He unclasped the back and stepped back to watch it fall between them.

Her nipples ached for his touch, they seemed to reach for him, urging him to take them. With one hand, he cupped a breast and his thumb pressed into the apricot colored nub, and with the other, he pinched, then twisted. Madeline leaned back moaning with desire. Ewan took her nipple into his mouth, biting playfully. She fell onto the bed then, they both did really.

He slipped his fingers into the elastic of her panties. She lifted her hips so he could slide them off, which he did and tossed to the side of the room. He would take his time. She knew he would make sure she had come before he had his way with her.

Ewan put his hands on her knees. She wanted him to see all of her, so she let them drop opening herself to him. She was ready for the slightest touch, for his touch. He looked at her with a breath-taking intensity. He slipped two fingers inside of her, pressing up into her g-spot while his thumb twirled around her clit. She could barely take it and bucked against his hand. Draping one arm across her stomach to stop her grinding hips, he withdrew his fingers and sucked on them. Watching him taste her, watching his expression change to that of want, made her wet with mad desire.

His head disappeared between her thighs, but she didn't feel anything yet and used the moment to catch up on her breath. With two fingers he swirled around her pubis and around her outer labia. Her body ached, she wanted to thrust against him, but his arm reminded her to be still. The want began to fill her, fast and hard. She needed him to take her clit into his mouth, to release all this tension, to satisfy her.

"Take me Ewan!" she cried out, unable to wait.

"Not yet, Love." He got on his knees and slipped his hand under her bottom. She raised her hips high to meet his mouth. With his tongue, he circled around her clit, tighter and tighter until he took the whole nub of her into his mouth, and sucked hard, releasing, then sucking again.

Madeline gasped for air, as if there were none left in the room at all. She clutched the bedspread and thrust her hips higher. With his other hand, fingers reached inside her, pulsing, his tongue grinding against her clit.

The pressure sent her reeling. It was as if she was suspended, floating on air, anchored only by his tongue, by his hands. Her pussy clenched as if she could hold onto him, but the rest of her body elongated and she stretched out to let the orgasm come, crashing through her like a strong wind. He pulled his hand away and released her. Her hips dropped to the bed, and he laid next to her, on his stomach, breathing hard.

"I could die now," she said under her breath, more to herself than to Ewan.

He rolled over, onto his back. "We're not even close to being finished," he said, nodding down to his erection.

"Am I to stay here all weekend?" she asked, propping herself up on an elbow to see how he reacted.

"Will you?" he asked, in all earnest. "Actually, I'd prefer it if you just moved your things in straight away, but, well, I don't want to scare you."

"You don't scare me." Madeline didn't think her

heart could pound any faster, but it did. "I will move in with you. My lease is up in a couple months."

"A couple months?" he asked, a grin spreading over his face. He rolled over on top of her. "What will you tell your sister?"

"Don't you worry about her." Madeline poked him gently in the ribs. "I'll tell her. I'm sure Dave clued her in."

"I hope so." He reached behind her neck and came in for an embrace. "I'm so glad I didn't get married. I would have missed out on this."

"Come here," she said, bringing him up for a deeper kiss.

"I want to touch every part of you." He rolled onto his back. She gasped, surprised by the force and was now sitting astride him.

"Like this?" she said, her head cocked, she put her hands down beside him and lifted her chest, brushing her nipples against his. He reached up to caress her breast and pinched her nipples.

"Is this what you want Ewan?"

"Yes," he said, trying to lift himself up. She pinned his hands down and leaned over him, her nipples hanging just above his mouth, his tongue barely able to reach. The light touches of his mouth teased her. He lifted his knee between her legs, and she ground her clitoris hard against him.

He thrust his hips, egging her on, demanding she give in.

She placed both her hands on his stomach, and he stopped moving. His hard penis was covered by her wet pussy, but not yet inside. She caressed the tip, letting her fingers follow the velvety soft crown around while sliding her hips back and forth over him.

Ewan tilted his head back and groaned.

"Watch," she said.

His eyes opened. She stood up on her knees and pulled his cock back. His hands wrapped around her hips. Without letting her go and without looking away, he shifted his hips to adjust himself. His tip found her opening. She slid down on him the entire length and girth of his cock filling her. She arched her back with a loud moan as he stretched her tight pussy open, enveloping him into her body.

She was half gone with the exquisite pleasure of having him inside her. She saw her reflection in the endless depth of his blue eyes.

"We were meant for each other." His voice was a low, hungry growl.

"I belong to you." She squeezed her pussy around his cock.

"I'll take what's mine." He grabbed her waist and pulled her down even further. His cock stretched her wide and touched her core at the same time.

She thrust her hips forward, hungrily finding a steady rhythm. They moved in sync, their bodies unable to separate. Harder, and faster, they kept pace with each other. His dick quivered with the chaos that comes before ejaculation. His eyes closed, and she rode him, her hips sweeping back and forth. His body stiffened and his face contorted with the throes of passion. Madeline arched her back. Suddenly, she fell, fell, fell into the depth of oblivion as if she'd been tossed over a cliff, losing herself in a passionate climax that shook both of them.

She collapsed on top of him, letting her chest rest on his. His hands roved over her back, her buttocks, her thighs. Like he was claiming her, and calming her with the knowledge that he was as much hers as she was his.

The room smelled musky with sex. Soft music played in the background. The stars shone brightly and the full moon appeared to be right outside the window. He wrapped his arms around her waist and pulled her body next to him. His hand ran down the length of her, curving around her buttocks, dipping into the curve of her waist, under the swelling of her breast.

"I belong to you." He kissed her sweetly, with his arms wrapped around her. "I'm never letting you go," he said. "Not now, and not in a million years."

"Like either of us had a choice in the whole matter."

"But you did. You could have said *no* that you didn't want to meet me. You could have told me you wouldn't wait. All of those were choices, Madeline. What is happening here... is because we both chose."

"I meant that we didn't decide to meet each other in the Hamptons. And tonight. We were supposed to meet tomorrow, but, voila, fate intervened, and we ran into each other tonight. Yes, we chose each other, but fate had a turn too."

"You believe *me* to be your fate?"

"I do." She said it without any hesitation. She brushed a finger over his eyebrow.

They lay face to face and breathed into one another. He pulled her palm between them and kissed each tip of her finger. She loved the feeling of his skin on hers. When he pulled out, she was sad to have him go. But before going to sleep, she threw all the extra pillows off the bed, and wrapped her arms and legs around him, holding onto the one man who made her want to throw all logic away, the one man who made blue skies even more blue.

More by Juno Chase

The DC Knights series can be read in any order, but we hope you don't miss any of them!

New to the Game—D.C. Knights Book 1

Chloe's the new intern, but she jumps into the game both feet first.

Playing For Keeps—D.C. Knights Book 2

Katherine thinks she's got things figured out until a sexy scientist tangos his way into her heart.

All In—D.C. Knights Book 3

Madeline has no problem playing games until she meets Ewan a man who knows how to treat her like a woman.

Fair and Square—D.C. Knights Book 4

Lizbeth doesn't have time for games, but she ends up in the midst of a political game no one in Congressman Pierce's office saw coming.

Only Bluffing—D.C. Knights Book 5

Eleanor Winslow and Daniel Prado are from different worlds. Will their love overcome dark histories and ancient legacies?

Game On—D.C. Knights Book 6

Cheyenne LeFleur lives on the wild side. Will Alexander Moore be able to handle her history, or will he reject her like so many before him?

For the Win—D.C. Knights Book 7 The final chapter in this series. Congressman Lincoln Pierce deserves love, too. Can he find it while maintaining his principles?

Also by Juno Chase:

ARTIFACT of BETRAYAL: an exciting romantic suspense novel

If you had to choose between saving your life or the love of your life, *who would you choose?*

Claire Townsend has it all, a great job, her own shop in Brooklyn, until one night when she loses everything. With thirteen days to pay off a dangerous loan shark, she decides to partake in a black-market smuggling operation to save her own neck.

Bruno Canul is an archeologist who works as a consultant with the FBI. He chases a suspect to Belize only to find the ex-love-of-his-life as part of the crew. He can't tell if he should trust Claire or if she's joined forces with the smuggler.

Afraid her choices will get Bruno killed, Claire tries to resist falling back in love with him. If she goes through with the smuggling scheme, she can pay off her loan, but she'd lose Bruno's love and trust *forever*. If she stands up for their love, she's a dead woman.

This adventurous romantic suspense is sure to keep you on the edge of your seat as Claire and Bruno find love in the jungle and ancient Mayan ruins of Belize.

About Juno Chase

Who said chivalry is dead? They were totally wrong! We love, love, love hot guys who are modern day knights and heroes but also know how to heat things up between the sheets.

Juno Chase is the nom de plume of two married moms who love reading and writing happy stories. We wanted to see these modern day knights celebrated in romance, so here we are. We're not a big group of people writing—there is just the two of us. We both spend lots of time reading and writing in each story to bring you the most complete, hot, and exciting stories possible.

Thank you so much for reading *New to the Game*, we hope you enjoyed reading it as much as we did writing it. If you sign up for our newsletter, you will be the first to know whenever we have a new book available.

Follow Juno Chase on your favorite social Media. We'd love to hear from you!

www.Junochase.com

juno@junochase.com

Acknowledgments

We'd like to thank a few people who helped us get this book into your lovely hands, dear readers. We are part of an amazing writing group who has listened to our ideas, helped us with plotting, and given us some straight feedback. We couldn't have done this without your energy and help-—you ladies rock! Thank you for all your reading time and thoughtful suggestions to help make the D.C. Knights series a reality.

To our intrepid beta readers. Thank you for taking the time to read and give us honest criticism. Especially to Dawn who has faithfully read everything we've handed her and keeps asking for more!

And to our families—our fabulous husbands and children who have supported us in so many different ways and picked up the pieces as needed. We love you!

www.ingramcontent.com/pod-product-compliance
Lightning Source LLC
Chambersburg PA
CBHW050508190726
48284CB00003B/734